OLD THINGS ARE PASSED AWAY

An Agape Love Story

By

Frieda Smith

This book is a work of fiction. Names, characters, and incidents are products of the author's imagination or are used fictitiously (with the exception of Elder Nicholas Soto; The Agape Christian Church; and the Mercy Seat Baptist Church). Any resemblance to actual events or persons— living or dead—is entirely coincidental.

To
Zaneta, Rachelle,
and
Isabella Rae

ACKNOWLEDGMENTS

It is with the utmost gratitude that I humbly thank God for depositing within me a wonderful imagination and the gift of writing to express it in print.

I wish to especially thank my beautiful and talented daughters, Zaneta and Rachelle; my sisters Curtarene, Ideluia and Kaori; my brothers DeVon and Dwight Sr.; my "son," Shaun Alexander; and my "Mom," Minister Alverta Bethea, for their continuous love, support, and encouragement.

A special thanks to Sister Chelsea Williams, the beloved wife of my Virginia Pastor, Reverend I. Charles Williams, Mercy Seat Baptist Church of Hampton, who graciously offered her proofreading gifts to me.

To my gifted, brilliant, and anointed cover artist, Elizabeth M. Tubman...may God bless you for graciously sharing your artistic talent with me.

To my Rehoboth VA family: I cannot thank you enough for your presence, encouragement and support during this exciting church planting season. Each of you inspire me to keep standing, keep moving forward, and keep proclaiming the Good News of the Gospel!

To my Rehoboth NY family: For those who have maintained a close relationship with me, your presence in my life has been a source of great joy. I love you all dearly, and am praying for you daily!

Last but never least, I wish to thank my Dad-In-The-Ministry, Bishop John H. Gilmore, for speaking one word that keeps me moving forward when I want to give up: Persevere; and my Mom-In-The-Ministry, Pastor Donna Lyn Smith Taylor, for taking me under your wing during my early years as a young female preacher. You taught me and so many others who were watching you how to "Act like a lady but preach like a man!"

The characters in this book were inspired by real people in my life; you know who you are because I already thanked you in private.

My friends, as you read this story of agape love, it is going to force you to evaluate your ability to love those of us who have led less-than-perfect lives as Jesus Christ loves us.

Some of you will pass the test easily; others will fail miserably.

Nevertheless, the Word of God is sure!

"If anyone is in Christ, he is a new creation. Old things are passed away; behold, all things are become new." 2nd Corinthians 5:17

1

"It's a shame you can't stay here, Paula. They did a beautiful job redesigning and rebuilding this townhouse after the fire. But, trust me, I do understand," Mia said to her younger sister as they sealed the last of the boxes in anticipation of the arrival of the moving company.

"I tried, Mia, I really did. But I just can't get comfortable. It is hard for me to sleep at night. Every time I hear a siren in the distance, I swear the fire trucks are on their way here. I know I'm probably imagining things, but I can still smell a slight scent of the smoke that engulfed this place three years ago," Paula stated with sadness in her eyes.

Mia fully understood. She vividly recalled the night she and her sister fled from a jazz concert to the devastating fire that totally destroyed Paula's townhouse. The only good thing that resulted from that fateful evening was her meeting Jayson Stewart.

I wonder how he and Syrene are doing? Mia thought.

Absentmindedly, Mia shook her head as if she could shake the memory of her former fiancé. However, she knew it would take a while for that to happen, if ever.

Never in her life had she sacrificed as much for a man; yet, she still believed in her heart she did the right thing in letting him go.

Paula's voice reclaimed Mia's attention.

"Can you stay here for about an hour while I go to the post office to get a change-of-address card?"

"Can't you change your address online these days?" Mia asked.

"Yes, I can, but I don't have internet access anymore. I had the cable turned off already," Paula replied.

"No problem, Paula, I don't have anywhere to go until later this afternoon," Mia answered.

"Oh really? What do you have going on?" Paula asked, her eyebrows raised, as if her sister had been holding out on some juicy information.

"It's not what you think, Paula," Mia said with a smile. "The prison ministry at our church is going to the county jail tonight to host a service. I usually don't go, being a federal probation officer, but Reverend Holloway asked the choir to sing during the service."

"I think it will be good for you, seeing offenders from a different perspective," Paula said. "You've always seen them on official business. This evening you will get to see them as your brothers and sisters in Christ."

Mia shook her headful of unruly curls in disagreement and said, "Believe me when I tell you, Sis, they will always be criminals to me. I know what they say and how they act when they are in jail. They all swear on their grandmother's graves that they'll never commit another crime when they get out. Even the ones who attend the services at the jail swear they will join a church as soon as they get released. But ask me how many of them follow through? I've been an officer for nine years now, and I can count the sincere ones with seven fingers! That's part of the reason why I don't like doing prison ministry. It's a waste of my valuable time!"

Paula looked at her sister as if she were a stranger.

"What's gotten into you, Mia? I'm really surprised to hear you talking like that. They're the people who need the Gospel more than the ones who show up for the 'Sunday morning fashion show' every week!"

Paula is right, Mia admitted. She had to confess her perspective had shifted after Jayson and Syrene's marriage. Perhaps it was because she had not fully come to terms with the loss of her best friend and fiancé.

Furthermore, to avoid controversy and uneasiness for Jayson and Syrene, Mia left the church after their wedding and found another church home.

As Paula rushed out the front door, headed to the post office, Mia sat on Paula's living room couch. She glanced around the townhouse that had been her home when she first relocated from Harlem, NY to Hampton, VA.

She recalled the warmth she enjoyed while sitting in front of Paula's fireplace, listening to the crackling wood and watching the tongues of the flames slowly consume everything in its path.

Now, with everything packed away in boxes, the townhouse looked as barren as Mia's life.

Paula is making a change by moving...maybe I need to make some moves as well, Mia thought.

Mia's cell phone rang.

She looked at the caller ID. It was Reverend Frank Holloway, the leader of the prison ministry.

"Good afternoon, Reverend," Mia spoke into the phone, trying her best to sound interested.

"Good afternoon, Sister Mia," Reverend Holloway replied. *"How are you doing today?"*

Mia could envision him with his smooth voice, light brown eyes, perfect teeth, handsome face, medium-brown complexion, and six-foot four frame smiling into the mouthpiece of his phone.

Reverend Holloway was *"eye-candy"* to most women, but Mia Wells was not like most women.

A proud native of the great state of New York and a college-educated federal probation officer, Mia was not enchanted by the looks or charms of men in whom she came in contact. She was never the type of woman to have to beg for attention; rather, it found its way to her everywhere she went.

Her hair attracted the most attention. Thick, big, black, natural curls dominated her head. As a result, Mia came to detest family gatherings, because while her younger sister and other female cousins were allowed to play and enjoy themselves, she always found herself parked on someone's lap or sitting on the floor between her mother's, aunt's, or female cousin's knees because they—armed with combs, brushes, and hair grease—were determined to bring some type of order to the chaos atop of Mia's head.

Nevertheless, her unruly curls stood their ground like a mighty oak.

Mia was an attractive, rich-chocolate, and ample woman with a captivating personality to match. Her stylish attire was always complimentary of her extra-large frame.

In other words, Mia graduated from the school of *"I-know-I-am-a-size-20-so-I-am-not-trying-to-squeeze-my-hips-into-a-size-14!"*

Already tall, Mia nonetheless wore heels that easily sent her height soaring over six-feet, and she loved to wear bright colors an insecure woman would never have the audacity to put on.

Mia Wells was a woman who was sure of herself.

From what Mia observed about Reverend Holloway, he was sincere about ministry. Although he was single, he was in a committed relationship with one of the members of the prayer ministry.

In all fairness to him, it wasn't his fault that God created such a beautiful specimen of a man.

"So, I heard you will be joining us this evening for our monthly service at the County Jail," Reverend Holloway stated, bringing Mia's thoughts back to the conversation.

"Yes I will. We're scheduled to leave the church at four o'clock on the van. I told the choir members to bring as little as possible because they won't be permitted to enter the jail with their big pocketbooks," Mia said.

"Thank you, Sister Mia. I really appreciate your willingness to assist the prison ministry. You may not know this—being that you just joined Wayside less than a year ago—but I'm a former drug dealer who was in and out of that same jail on a regular basis. But one day while

14

I was locked up, I attended a service, got saved, and joined Wayside as soon as I was released. I have been saved and crime-free for eleven years, so I know the true value of prison ministry firsthand. My life was turned around because of it."

Wow, Mia said to herself, *I had no idea. You would never know his past looking at him now. I guess he's a living example of what the Apostle Paul wrote in 2nd Corinthians 5:17: "Old things are passed away; behold, all things have become new."*

"That's quite a testimony you have, Reverend Holloway. Thank God for your deliverance, and your willingness to help those who are still lost. After listening to your testimony, I really look forward to the service tonight," Mia said.

"Thank you. Oh, and one last thing. Please let your choir members know that we hold the names and identities of all inmates who we meet in the strictest of confidence, and especially those who attend our church after their release. We never disclose to the membership the criminal past of

15

the inmates we minister to. They deserve to be treated with dignity and respect when they are released and come to Wayside."

"That's not a problem, Reverend Holloway. Being a federal probation officer, I am very familiar with the need for and importance of confidentiality. I'll be sure to pass this information to the choir as well," Mia said.

"Thank you, Sister Mia. I will see you this evening at the jail," Reverend Holloway said.

As she disconnected the call and placed her phone on top of her sister's end table, Mia paused to think about her own life.

Once a carefree woman, she had become skeptical and judgmental of people around her, especially those she felt were still "worldly".

I have no right to pass judgment on others, Mia reflected.

No one is perfect. I have to do better.

Old things have passed away.

2

Mia saw the raised hood of the van as soon as she drove her car onto the church's parking lot.

Several of her choir members stood huddled nearby in small groups, talking among themselves.

"What is the problem?" Mia asked as she rushed to the van, checking her wristwatch.

The head of the transportation ministry, Brother Rogers, lifted his head from underneath the hood. Beads of sweat rolled down his face. He wiped them with a small brown washcloth he removed from the pocket of his pants.

"I don't know, Sister Mia. It was running fine yesterday. It's probably the alternator," he said, shaking his head.

Mia looked at her watch again and then back at their church's van. It wasn't an antique, but it certainly had seen better days.

There was no way the van was pulling out of the parking lot in time for their singing engagement at the jail.

Walking over to where her choir members were huddled, Mia said, *"It looks like the van is not going to be able to take us to the jail. I can drive and take some members. Are there any more volunteers?"*

The murmuring began. Several choir members looked at each other, while others rolled their eyes or sucked their teeth.

Denise Addison spoke first. *"I don't mind driving, but I don't have enough gas to get to the jail and back. I'm on 'E' and my gas indicator light is on. I fasted and prayed all the way over here."*

"Quit lyin', Denise. You ain't on a fast. We stopped at Happy Burger on the way over here. You put your gas money in your stomach," Tamara Campbell announced.

"That's not a problem, Denise," Mia replied with a laugh. "We will give you gas money to drive to the jail. Anybody else willing to drive? We need two more volunteers. We have twenty choir members to transport."

The choir members with cars continued to stare at Mia. No one else volunteered.

I cannot believe these people, Mia thought.

Mia heard the sound of gravel as two of her tenors—Daryl Walker and Brian Morgan—drove into the parking lot.

"What's going on, Mia?" Daryl asked, the sun reflecting off his baldhead as he leaned through the open driver's side window.

"The church van broke down and we need two more drivers in order to get all the choir members to the jail," Mia explained.

Daryl said, *"I'll drive."*

Brian spoke up as well. *"I'll go back and get my car if you need me to. I live three blocks away."*

For a moment, Mia turned in the direction of her huddled choir members. Their faces had not changed. The murmuring, eye rolling, and teeth sucking had not stopped.

I should leave them right here out of spite, Mia considered.

In retrospect, however, she thought otherwise.

"Thanks. Brian, we'll wait here until you get back."

"No problem, Mia. We'll be right back," Daryl said, smiling at her as he ducked his shiny head back inside the car and hurried out of the parking lot in the direction of Brian's house.

Reluctantly, Mia walked over to the choir members who were still huddled in small groups. She quickly performed an inspection of their attire, as she specifically instructed the women not to wear clothing that was too tight or revealing. Most of her choir members complied; however, there was always one.

Darlene Walker dressed as if she was booked for a photo shoot for an international magazine cover.

While Mia was modestly dressed in a calf-length denim skirt, topped with a pale blue open collar blouse and flat sandals, Darlene appeared to have walked out of a high-end boutique on Park Avenue in New York City.

For their trip to the county jail, Darlene's shoulder-length hair was flat-ironed straight and parted on the side, revealing dangling gold earrings. She selected a gold-colored denim outfit that hugged her generous curves. Underneath the jacket, she wore a floral camisole she must have purchased at a lingerie shop. She sported gold-toned, three-inch high-heeled sandals on her bare but pedicured feet and two gold rings donned her long manicured fingernails.

Meticulously-applied makeup and overpowering perfume completed the package.

Lord help us today, Mia muttered, shaking her head. *There's always one!*

Mia turned her attention back to the choir.

"As soon as Brian and Daryl get back, we're going to have to load up quickly so we can get to the jail and go through security in time for the service."

Georgia Lindsay spoke up.

"Sister Mia, I can't speak for anybody else, but I didn't feel like going in the first place. The only reason I'm here is because I hold up the entire soprano section. But now with all the drama going on with transportation, I'd rather go home."

Georgia looked around at her friends for support. Several of them nodded in agreement, while others just resumed murmuring in their small groups, oblivious to what had just been said.

Mia viewed Georgia's arrogance with disdain, and replied, *"Georgia, you're free to leave. Honestly, I'd prefer if you did. We don't need to be taking any negative spirits into the jail; we'll have our hands full combating the demons that are already there."*

"Oh, and about holding up the entire soprano section and the choir needing you—that's where you're wrong!" Mia said. *"Grace and I can sing soprano, alto, and tenor, so if you go home, the choir won't fall apart!"*

The murmuring ceased. Every head turned in the direction of Georgia, waiting for a response. When none came after several seconds, Mia turned to the rest of the choir members still huddled in their small groups.

"Does anyone else want to leave?" Mia asked.

Georgia turned to her friends, her eyes pleading for them to join in her revolt.

No one moved. No one said a word, especially Darlene Walker.

The trip to the jail was obviously the highlight of her week.

Just as Georgia was about to turn and walk to her car, Brian and Daryl pulled into the parking lot.

The little huddles quickly disbanded. Darlene Walker took off running in her three-inch high heels toward her brother's car as if someone fired the starter's pistol for the one hundred meter dash. The remaining choir members scattered and began loading into the cars.

Mia turned to Georgia. The arrogance that had been in Georgia's demeanor moments prior was no longer there. In its place was remorse for her earlier self-exalting proclamation.

Walking over to her lead soprano, Mia said, *"Georgia, I understand that you don't want to go. Quiet as it's kept, I am not in love with the idea either. However, this is ministry. It's what Jesus instructed us to do. You said you didn't want to go, but it's okay to change your mind."*

Georgia looked at Mia and then at her fellow choir members climbing into cars. She turned to Mia and asked, *"Who's riding in your car?"*

Mia smiled and responded, *"You are,"* as she grabbed Georgia's arm, turned and walked toward her car.

3

The caravan of cars from Wayside pulled into the county jail parking lot, and the choir members immediately exited their vehicles.

It was visiting day at the jail; so, there was a long line of people baking in the late afternoon sun, waiting for their turn in front of the cranky corrections officer who sat in the air-conditioned, brick-covered booth with bulletproof glass.

Mia gathered the choir members together in the parking lot.

"You all wait here. I'll go to the front of the line, tell the officer who we are and our purpose for being here, and once we're cleared to enter, I'll motion for you all to join me. Just be ready to move at my signal," Mia said.

"We'll be praying that you get to the front of that line in one piece," Georgia said half-jokingly while looking at all the people who were already waiting.

Reality sunk in. Georgia had a point.

"Pray hard, saints. This is going to be a tough crowd," Mia sighed as she left the choir members and headed toward the line.

Lord knows I do not want to have to cut this line, but oh well, Mia said to herself as she smiled and politely said, "Excuse me," as she made her way past sweaty and disgruntled family and friends of the inmates to the front of the line.

As predicted, an inattentive, frustrated, and cranky corrections officer manned the booth.

"Didn't you notice that line out there?" he barked.

Mia inhaled deeply, smiled, and said, "Good evening Officer. My name is Mia Wells, and I am the choir director *from Wayside Christian Temple. We're here for our monthly outreach service at five o'clock this evening."*

The inattentive, frustrated, and cranky corrections officer behind the air-conditioned booth was not impressed, but nonetheless began looking through a stack of papers attached to a worn clipboard on his desk.

"What church was that?" he asked rudely, squinting through thick black-rimmed bifocals perched on the edge of his big nose.

"Wayside Christian Temple," Mia said a little louder as she peered through the bulletproof glass at the papers, trying her best to read upside down.

"Here it is," the corrections officer said as he snatched a single sheet off of the clipboard, leaving the jagged top portion still attached.

"Does everyone have ID?" he snarled.

"Yes sir," Mia said.

"Lemme see yours," the correction officer demanded.

Mia reached in her purse and produced her driver's license, exposing her Federal Probation Officer's shield.

The scowl that had covered the cranky correction officer's face suddenly vanished.

"How long you been on the job?" he asked.

"Nine years in August," Mia replied.

"Are they hiring over there? This place is the pits," he said.

If your attitude is any indication, I can tell, Mia mumbled to herself.

Mia smiled, *"I'm not sure. Go online and complete an application. There's probably a test coming up soon."*

"Thanks. Where are the rest of the people in your group?" the officer asked, looking over her shoulder.

"In the parking lot," Mia said, as she turned and waved to her choir members to join her in the front of the line.

Darlene Walker took off running as if she heard the starter's pistol for the two hundred meter dash. She stepped on Denise Addison's foot in the process. Denise shrieked in agony. Darlene apologized over her shoulder, but did not slow down until she joined Mia in the front of the line.

Darlene must've been a track star back in the day, Mia said to herself.

Several people who had been waiting patiently in the long line, sweltering in the hot sun, had enough.

"Wait a minute! What the heck is going on?" someone shouted angrily, refusing to step aside. *"Why are these people cutting the line?"*

The corrections officer's voice boomed through the speakers as he spoke through a microphone in the booth where he stood.   Surprisingly, he maintained his composure in the midst of the small riot that was about to break out in front of his booth.

"Look people. This is a group of singers from a church that is coming in for a worship service at five o'clock. Everyone step to the left and let them through so I can quickly check them in. Don't worry; you all will still have plenty of time for your visits."

Remarkably, the crowd obediently stepped to the left as Mia's choir members apologetically walked past (with the exception of Denise Addison who was limping) and presented their ID's to the officer.

When they were cleared to enter, he pressed a big red button on the side of the wall, and the door buzzed. Mia pushed the door open, and they all walked through.

With the exception of Denise Addison, who limped through.

Mia looked at her watch; it was four-forty p.m. They had twenty minutes to get through the security check and set up for the service that was to begin at five p.m.

She hustled the choir members up the walkway and steps leading to the main entrance of the jail. There were lockers on the right, where she instructed the choir members to secure their personal belongings.

She approached the officers who manned the entry station and showed them her identification.

"Good afternoon officers. My name is Mia Wells, and we are the singers from Wayside Christian Temple. We are here for a service tonight with Reverend Holloway."

"Good evening, Officer Wells. I'm Officer Franklin. What time is the service tonight?" he asked.

"Five o'clock," Mia said.

Officer Franklin picked up a piece of paper on his desk and handed it to Mia.

"Is there anyone in your group whose name is not on this list?" he asked.

Mia scanned the names and turned in the direction of her choir members. Out of the corner of her eye, she saw Darlene Walker trying to cram an overstuffed pocketbook into the narrow locker.

Didn't I tell them to leave their big pocketbooks home? Goodness gracious! Mia said to herself with aggravation.

"Everyone here is on the list," Mia said.

"Great. We'll start calling their names one by one. They need their ID with them at all times. After signing in, they'll have to pass through the metal detectors. You know the drill," the Officer Franklin said.

"Unfortunately, I do," Mia said.

When she first joined the federal probation department, all she needed to do was show her shield to the officer at the booth, and they would buzz her in without question.

Apparently, one of her fellow law enforcement officers must have messed it up for everyone, because now even she had to walk through the metal detectors just like the general public.

Officer Franklin called the names of the choir members, and they walked through the metal detector without incident, except poor Denise Addison of course. She limped through.

Mia was last to go through the detector. She put her shield, watch, and belt on the table next to the metal detector.

She slowly walked through.

The alarm sounded.

"Step back and walk through again," Officer Franklin said.

Mia walked back out and stepped through a second time.

The alarm sounded again.

"Officer Wells, is there anything you neglected to remove from your pockets? Are there pins in your hair perhaps?" Officer Franklin asked.

Mia suspected what was happening, although her choir members did not.

She walked to her locker, removed her wallet, and located a card. She handed it to Officer Franklin, who looked at her with a tinge of compassion.

"You should have said something earlier," he said. *"We could have bypassed this altogether."*

"I know, Officer. I just wanted to fit in just like everyone else," Mia replied.

"Lift up your head, Sis. It's all right. All of us have some kind of issue. At least you have a device to treat yours," he said. *"Imagine what some of these inmates go through*

on a daily basis. No one has manufactured a device to treat stupidity."

"You have a point, Officer Franklin" Mia laughed.

Mia passed through the metal detector a third time. The alarm sounded, but she kept walking with her head held high.

Darlene Walker asked the question the rest wished they had the nerve to.

"What was that about, Mia?"

"The metal detector went off because it isn't programmed to handle my anointing," Mia replied.

"You are too much, Mia," Darlene laughed.

Mia and her choir members followed their escort down a long hallway, made several turns, and continued to walk through a maze of hallways.

Several inmates spotted them, began whistling, and calling out to them, particularly to Darlene Walker.

"Hey! Hey!" they shouted. *"You with the gold suit!"*

Mia and her entourage ignored them and kept walking. Darlene tried her best to appear unperturbed but failed miserably.

A door buzzed open in front of them, which led to a very large room. The inmates had begun to gather for the service. Some were lining up chairs, while others were connecting the portable keyboard to the correction facility's sound system.

Several inmates seated in the back of the room were looking disinterested, as if their sole purpose for being there was to get out of their cell for an hour or so.

Two inmates rolled a dolly that bore a drum set across the concrete floor. After carefully unloading it, they assembled the set near the electronic keyboard.

Nice setup for a jail, Mia pondered. *This sound system appears better than the one at the church.*

She spotted Reverend Holloway in the front of the room, removing his Bible and note pad from his briefcase. As she approached him, he looked up and beamed.

"Mia! You all had me worried for a moment. I was beginning to think you changed your mind," he said.

"Never, Reverend Holloway. The church van broke down in the parking lot so we had to wait for one of our members to go back and get his car. We're here now, ready to sing," Mia answered with a smile.

She looked around and said, *"Where would you like the choir to stand when they sing?"*

Reverend Holloway replied, *"I'm going to leave that up to you, Sister Mia. By the way, the service is only an hour. I'll open the service with prayer and scripture, and the choir can sing two selections and then I will bring the*

Word. Afterward, play a song of invitation. I'm believing God that someone will accept Jesus as Lord during this service."

"Amen, Reverend Holloway. I believe so, too. I'm going to seat the choir members in the front rows over there," she said, pointing to the section near the keyboard.

After doing so, Mia sat on the piano bench and turned on the keyboard.

An inmate walked up to her.

"Hi. Do you have a drummer?" he asked.

Mia looked up from the keyboard into the face of a handsome man, who appeared to be in his early thirties. Covering his brown eyes were the most beautiful eyelashes Mia had even seen on a man. His brown face bore the invisible scars of life on the streets, yet there was something different about him. He was unlike many of the criminal's Mia encountered in her line of work.

"No, I don't. Do you know how to play?" Mia asked bluntly.

The last thing I need is some wannabe drummer unable to maintain a steady beat and messing us up tonight, she thought to herself.

"Yes I do. I played at my father's church ever since I was a little kid," he replied.

He extended his right hand. "Jackson Braynor."

She shook his hand. "Mia Wells. Nice to meet you and thank you for offering to help us out this evening."

"No problem Miss Wells. What church is here?" Jackson asked as he sat on the stool and reached for the drumsticks.

As Mia was about to answer him, she heard the voice of Reverend Holloway speaking through the sound system, directing the attention of the inmates to Psalm 150. Mia began playing music softly and led the choir in the singing of the opening selection, "Glory To Your Name!"

As the music began filling the large room, from Mia's seat she noticed how the inmates started getting involved in the worship experience. Some of them stood with their eyes closed and their hands extended toward the ceiling. Others sat alone in the corner with their heads bowed. The sightseers in the back of the room even started paying attention, unsure of what they had gotten themselves into.

Wow, she thought. *Most of them look like they are really serious about this. This may not be a waste after all.*

As soon as the thought left Mia's mind, she heard a familiar Voice speaking to her spirit.

No life is a waste to Me.

Old things are passed away. Behold!

All things are become new.

4

At the conclusion of the worship service, Mia turned to the drummer.

"Jackson, thanks for helping us out this evening. You're really good. I hope whenever you are released, you will return to your father's church and continue to serve in the music ministry."

"Thank you for allowing me to play with you and your choir," Jackson said, as he began to disassemble the drum set.

"Where is your church located, because to be honest, I'm no longer welcome at my father's church. He's pretty much done with me. This is my fifth time getting locked up," Jackson said sadly.

"What are you in here for?" Mia asked as she scribbled the name and address of Wayside on a piece of paper.

"*This time, I'm in here on two different charges. One for possession of marijuana and the other for stealing money out of the offering basket when they passed it around,*" Jackson said.

"*Jackson, I can't blame your father for having you arrested. You have to be accountable for your actions, otherwise, nothing will ever change,*" Mia said. "*How much time do you have left to serve on your sentence, and what are your plans once you get out?*"

"*I'm finally attending the substance abuse program here at the jail. Also, I'm working on getting my GED. I was sentenced to a year for stealing the offering, and probation for the drug charge. I won't be released until the end of next month. Regardless, I want to get my life together. I don't want to be in and out of here for the rest of my life.*"

"*We all have choices, Jackson. You made a good one by attending the service on tonight,*" Mia said. "*Keep coming to the services here at the jail, focus on doing what you have been taught by your father, and make sure you find a church home when you are released. You need to surround yourself with a different group of people. As I'm sure you know, being a preacher's kid, church people have issues just like everyone else, but the difference is we have Jesus Christ, and we're supposed to try to help each other overcome our problems rather than wallow in them."*

"You're right, Sister Mia. I'm definitely going to visit your church when I'm released. I promise," Jackson said.

Yeah, that's what they all say, Mia said to herself.

"Well then let me introduce you to Reverend Holloway," Mia said as she walked in his direction. *"He's over the prison ministry at our church. He will keep in contact with you while you are still here, and will help you once you are released."*

Engrossed in a conversation with several inmates, Reverend Holloway turned when Mia lightly tapped his shoulder.

"Reverend, this is Jackson Braynor and he expressed an interest in attending Wayside once he is released," she said.

A huge smile engulfed Reverend Holloway's face. He extended his hand toward Jackson.

"Good evening, Brother Jackson. So nice to meet you. We would be honored if you came to Wayside after your release. I can also arrange to visit you on a weekly basis if you'd like so we can help coordinate any treatment or housing needs upon your release. Leave me your name, home address, and a number where you can be reached," Reverend Holloway said.

Jackson smiled in Mia's direction; she nodded her head in support.

"Thank you, Reverend for the word tonight. It really helped me. I also appreciate the invitation to attend the church after I'm released. I know for a fact that people such as myself aren't welcome in every church," Jackson said.

"Well, you will be welcomed with open arms at Wayside Christian Temple. You see, I used to spend a lot of time here myself, and not as a Correction Officer either. I was in and out of this place, probably just like you, until I attended one of these services and gave my life to the Lord. Now, I come in here once a month, to give those who are still incarcerated the Word of God that delivered me," Reverend Holloway said.

A ray of hope shone upon Jackson's face, as he wrote his contact information on a piece of paper.

"Please keep in touch with me, Reverend. I'm serious. I am sick and tired of the life I've been living. I know better. I was raised in the church. My father is a good man; he's a pastor. I became rebellious and now I'm paying for my failures. I promise if you give me your time, I won't waste it," Jackson pleaded.

"I believe you, Jackson, and I'll do all I can to help you get your life back on track. I'll be in touch," Reverend

Holloway said as he deposited Jackson's contact information in his briefcase.

"Thank you, sir. I have to go now, otherwise, I'll miss dinner," Jackson said.

"God bless, my brother, and thanks again for playing tonight," Reverend Holloway said as Mia headed in the direction of her choir members who were waiting for her at the door.

Mia's timing was perfect, for as she walked toward her choir members, she noticed that Darlene Walker was nowhere to be found.

She looked around and spotted Darlene huddled in a corner, absorbed in what appeared to be a very private conversation with an inmate.

The inmate was a little too close, and Darlene looked a little too spellbound.

Mia called to her.

"Excuse me, Darlene. Can I speak with you for a moment?"

Darlene frowned at Mia and waved her away. The inmate continued to grin as he whispered in her ear, and Darlene's smile broadened.

Oh no she didn't! Mia said to herself as she walked over and lightly tugged on Darlene's arm.

"Sister Darlene, may I speak with you for a minute?" Mia repeated, this time with a bit of annoyance in her voice.

"This is important, Sister Mia," Darlene insisted. *"He wanted to know if he could call me so we can talk about the Bible."*

Who is she trying to kid? Mia said to herself. *Darlene did not have an 'I-can't-wait-until-you-call-me-so-we-can-talk-about-the-Bible' look in her eyes!*

"Come on, Darlene," Mia said as she gently shoved Darlene toward the rest of the choir members who were

patiently waiting for Reverend Holloway to join them so they could be escorted out of the jail.

"It was a pleasure meeting you, young man," Mia shouted over her shoulder, as Reverend Holloway approached the rest of the group.

"My sisters and brothers, thank you so very much for your time this evening. You were a blessing to these young men. Your music ministry very well may have sent several of these men onto a different path tonight. Again, on behalf of all those who are incarcerated, thank you for caring enough to share your time and gifts tonight," he said.

Mia spoke on behalf of the choir.

"It was a great service, Reverend Holloway. We enjoyed ourselves, didn't we?"

All of the choir members nodded in agreement, except Darlene Walker, who was too busy searching the dispersing group of inmates for her supposed *"Bible study"* partner.

"Well, get home safely, and hopefully you didn't give everything you had tonight. You still have to sing tomorrow morning," he added.

"Oh, you never have to worry about that, Reverend Holloway. We always have something left over. We'll be ready to have church tomorrow," Mia said.

"That's what I'm talking about," Reverend Holloway said as a burly correction officer arrived, unlocked the door, and escorted them out of the building.

As the group made their way back to the parking lot, Mia thanked each of them personally for their time.

"It may not have meant much to you, but your being here to minister in music may have turned someone's life around tonight. I pray the Lord will bless each of you richly," Mia said.

Encouraged by her words, the choir members smiled and waved to Mia as they headed toward their cars.

5

After dropping Georgia off at the church to get her car, Mia stopped at the grocery store, picked up a prepackaged salad, a bag of potato chips, and drove straight to her apartment.

Her cell phone rang. She looked at the caller ID and answered.

"Hey Paula. What's going on?" Mia asked.

"The movers arrived about an hour late. We're just getting to my new townhouse. Can you believe this?" Paula said in disgust.

"I'm not surprised, Paula. It happens all the time. Do you need me to come over and help with anything?" Mia asked.

"I would love some help, but no. You have a long day tomorrow at church. I planned to go, but now I'll probably stay here and try to get things in order."

Paula continued, "How was the service at the jail? Did most your choir members show up? And what did Darlene Walker have on?"

Mia did her best to describe Darlene's inappropriate ensemble and the events of their evening at the jail as she drove through the gates of her apartment complex and parked in her assigned space.

Upon hearing of the "fashion show" Darlene put on and her private meeting with one of the inmates afterward, Paula said, "Why am I not surprised? I don't understand her. She doesn't need to do all of that. She's a natural beauty."

"It's probably a self-esteem issue," Mia answered. "There are some people who are never satisfied with themselves. They're always trying to look like someone else they believe is more attractive. Personally, I don't have time for all of that. For example, you've always been petite, while I've always been extra-large. I enjoy food too much to starve myself trying to look like you."

Paula replied, "It's funny, Mia. I've always envied you. You have so much confidence in yourself—it shows up as soon as you enter a room."

"It's nothing special, Paula. I have good self-esteem. I love who I am and how I look. To me, that's all that matters. Anyway, I'm home now and I'm about to get out of this car. Since we don't have an afternoon service tomorrow, I'll come over after church and help you unpack. Just make sure you unpack your pots and pans so dinner will be ready when I get there," Mia said with a laugh.

"I'll have a roast cooking in the slow cooker; it'll be ready when you get here. Have a good night, Sis. Love you," Paula said.

"Love you more," Mia replied as she disconnected the call.

Mia parked her car, walked to her front door, and entered the foyer of her apartment. It had been over three years since she moved in, but the fragrance and the appearance of the apartment remained fresh.

When a person entered Mia's apartment, they felt as if they were finally at home.

In retrospect, Mia had the same feeling when she entered Wayside Christian Temple after visiting with her coworker, Isabelle Jefferson.

It had been difficult leaving Unity Baptist after Jayson and Syrene's reunion and marriage. Mia loved Unity, and the people loved her. Mia believed she would never find the comfort she enjoyed at Unity Baptist.

Yet, after visiting several churches, she walked into Wayside one Sunday morning and found her new church home.

Unlike Unity Baptist, Wayside Christian Temple was a nondenominational congregation that had been planted less than fifteen years prior to Mia's arrival.

Housed in a one-story commercial building converted into a church, the exterior was painted white with gold trim. The front door was cherry-colored, and upon entering the vestibule of the church, parishioners walked on floral carpeting that represented every color in the rainbow.

A table was set up on the left of the entry with devotional materials. As Mia walked through the door of the main sanctuary, a pleasant usher—who was dressed from head to toe in white—smiled warmly as she handed Mia a visitor's packet and bulletin.

Instead of ushering Mia to a specific seat, the usher said, "*Sit wherever you feel comfortable.*"

Mia knew she was in a different church, because there was no "*sitting wherever you felt comfortable*" at Unity Baptist Church!

She remembered the day as if it was yesterday. She sat in an empty seat at Unity one Sunday morning, and received a call on her cell phone before she pulled out of the parking lot after church was over!

It was from the seat's *"owner,"* Mother Margarita Hawkins, who was home, recovering from major surgery.

"Do you mind tellin' me why you thought it was okay for you to sit in my seat this mornin'?" Mother Hawkins bellowed over the phone.

Mia stared at the phone, incredulously.

"Mother Hawkins. How are you feeling?" Mia responded, while holding onto the Holy Ghost for dear life.

"Don't be tryin' to change the subject, young lady. Er'body knows that's my seat you were sittin' in! Whether I'm there or not, that seat is mines!" Mother Hawkins said.

I just have to ask, Mia said to herself.

"Mother Hawkins? How did you know I was sitting in your seat?"

"I seent you in it wit my own two eyes! I was watchin' the service on TV, and the camera scanned the crowd and I looked to see if somebody was sittin' in my seat and there you wuz!" Mother Hawkins answered.

Lord help us today, Mia said to herself. You'd think the woman would be focused on the service. She only tuned in to see if someone would sit in her seat!

"I'm sorry if I upset you, Mother Hawkins. I hope you feel better," Mia said.

"I'll feel much betta when you keep your big behind outta of my seat!" she shouted before hanging up on Mia.

Mia chuckled at the memory as she and Isabelle found seats of their choosing and sat down.

While Unity Baptist boasted of a large membership, Wayside's membership numbered approximately ninety people; most of whom were close to Mia's age of thirty-two.

Surprisingly, the choir—although much smaller than Unity's—was amazing. There were only about thirteen of them, but they sounded as if there were thirty members.

Mia took her time and surveyed the sanctuary. Royal blue cloth-covered chairs were arranged in rows of fifteen, with a center aisle that led to the pulpit.

Positioned directly in front of the pulpit, was a communion table, with a white-covered Bible placed on top.

For a moment, her mind travelled further back to the day when she—as a little girl— made the deadly mistake of resting her little hand on top of the communion table.

"Mia Wells! You know better! Get your hands off the communion table!" Deaconess Banks scolded as she swiftly bolted from her second row pew to the table with a white handkerchief and wiped Mia's small fingerprints away.

Jeepers. I didn't know Deaconess Banks could move that fast. She always walked with a walker or a cane. That communion table must have power to heal, Mia recalled thinking on that Sunday morning.

Mia's mind returned to the recollection of her first Sunday at Wayside. Even though the pastor, Elder Jacob Rhodes, rose from his chair promptly at eleven a.m. for the call to worship, the rest of the worship service flowed in whatever direction the Holy Spirit took it and ended when it was over.

What Mia admired most was the diversity of the congregation. While Unity was somewhat *"stuffy,"* Wayside was laid-back and casual. People of all manner of dress, nationality, race, social status, and appearance were welcome as part of a wonderful family.

I really like it here, Mia mused. *I think Paula will, too.*

Mia was correct, because the following Sunday morning she brought Paula with her to Wayside, and when the pastor extended the invitation for membership, Paula left Mia sitting in her seat and went straight to the front.

I didn't know Paula could move that fast, either, Mia thought as she rose from her seat and joined her sister at the pastor's side in front of the church.

Since then, Paula attended church every Sunday. As a registered nurse, she joined the health ministry at the church, which provided free blood pressure and health screenings immediately after service on fourth Sundays in the fellowship hall.

Of course, Mia joined the music ministry, and within a month's time, she was the choir director. Under her leadership, the choir grew numerically and spiritually, as did the congregation, because word spread that Wayside Christian Temple had one of the best pastors and music ministries in the Hampton area.

Returning her thoughts to the present, Mia pulled up a chair to the island in her spacious kitchen and began to eat her salad and chips, while at the same time looking at various social media sites.

Momentarily, she entertained the thought of checking Jayson's social media pages. The last time she checked, Jayson, Syrene, and their son, J.J., were vacationing in the Bahamas, celebrating their first wedding anniversary.

That could have been me, Mia whispered longingly.

I have to move on. I made my decision and it was the right one, Mia assured herself as she deposited her salad plate in the dishwasher, and headed into her bedroom to ready herself for bed.

Mia placed her phone on the charger for the first time since she unplugged it earlier that morning. It dawned on her that her battery rarely died anymore.

No one was calling her.

A spirit of depression made a brief appearance.

She quickly said a prayer and it dispersed.

I'm okay, Mia convinced herself. *A little alone time is needed in order to prepare for God's next move.*

She stretched her long, ample body across her bed and turned out the lamp on her nightstand.

As her head touched the pillow and her eyes began to close, she could hear the Lord speaking.

Old things have passed away...

6

Mia arrived at her desk at the Federal Probation Department Monday morning at the same time her supervisor, Stacey Abraham, strode through the front door of their office.

As usual, Stacey breezed past Mia's desk without speaking, unlocked her office door, and slammed it behind her.

Stacey and Mia's working relationship started off poorly, and after three years, nothing had changed.

If anything, their relationship deteriorated after Stacey suspected that Mia somehow logged onto her computer and accessed information on Syrene Bookman, Jayson's former fiancé who had been placed in the Federal Witness Protection Program.

Due to the security breach, Stacey was severely reprimanded by her superiors. Although she knew Mia was somehow responsible, she could not prove it.

Stacey's office door opened and her voice thundered through the room.

"Wells. Get in here."

Mia looked across the aisle at Isabelle, who whispered, *"Mia, I don't know how you work with her. If she was my supervisor, I would probably be sitting in the waiting room by now, waiting to be seen by a probation officer after a felony conviction of assault. She's abusive. Why don't you report her to the union? Personally, I think she's racist."*

Mia stood and gathered a few papers from her desk.

"I don't know if it's a racial issue, Isabelle. I think she's just miserable and believes that after three years of unloading her garbage on me without any serious repercussions, it's okay. I don't take anything she says

personally. I know who I am and I know what I bring to my job every time I show up. Truthfully, she knows it, too. That's why she won't reassign me or allow me to transfer to another unit. Girl, let me get in there and see what she wants. I'll see you when I get back," Mia said.

Mia approached Stacey's door and knocked on the doorframe. She heard her usual command to enter.

"Good morning, Stacey!" Mia chirped, knowing her boisterous greeting would irk her grumpy supervisor.

"What's so good about it, Wells?" Stacey snapped.

"It's Monday morning and this is going to be a great week!" Mia proclaimed with her arms stretched wide.

"Sit down, Wells. I'm in no mood for your chirpiness this morning," Stacey snarled.

Mia watched as Stacey walked to a file cabinet and fumbled through the top drawer.

She would be a decent looking woman if she would lose the funky attitude and learn how to dress, Mia said to herself.

Stacey was a thin, Caucasian woman in her early forties. She was reasonably attractive, but lacked the knowledge, desire, or skill to polish her look. The permanent scowl on her face didn't help matters.

She needs to do something with her bleached blond hair; it is unflattering for her age. I'd like to take her on a shopping spree, too. Her clothes are outdated. She'll never find a man looking like that, and truthfully, that's what she needs, beside Jesus of course. With her bad attitude, it's apparent she hasn't found Him, either, Mia pondered.

Stacey turned quickly and caught Mia frowning in her direction.

"What the heck are you looking at?" Stacey barked.

Mia was caught. *I may as well come clean,* she said to herself.

"*Truthfully, I would not have chosen to wear those pants with that blouse. Your wardrobe needs some color, Stacey. When are you going to let me take you shopping?*"

"*Are you kidding me, Wells? I don't need your help with my wardrobe! I've been dressing myself for years, and since you seem to be the only one complaining, you must be the one with the problem, not me,*" Stacey said as she slammed several files on her desk and sat down. Her face darkened to the color of beets.

Stacey turned her attention to the business at hand.

"*Two of the officers in our unit are being promoted during the next two months. Since there's a federal hiring freeze, we will not be able to fill their vacated positions. Therefore, the offenders on their caseloads are being distributed throughout our unit. I need you to go through your files and apply for early discharges for any probationer who has been compliant for the past eighteen months to make room on your caseload for the offenders who will be reassigned to you."*

"I take it I'm not one of the officers who will be promoted," Mia said.

If looks could kill, Stacey would have been charged with first-degree murder, and taken out of her office in handcuffs.

The beet-red color in Stacey's face that had begun to wane was making a comeback.

"Are you serious, Wells? You just got here three years ago! The officers being promoted have been here for over twenty years," Stacey stated, her voice tinged with indignation.

"True, Stacey. But I didn't realize promotions were rewards for years of service; I thought they were merit-based," Mia said, struggling to maintain her Christian composure.

"*Like I told you when you first transferred to Virginia from New York, we do things differently down here,*" Stacey said, her face now flushed with anger and her voice beginning to match.

"*I see,*" Mia replied as she stood to leave. "*Will that be all, Stacey? I have interviews scheduled today.*"

"*Yeah, that's it. Close the door on your way out,*" Stacey demanded, waving her hand dismissively.

As was Mia's custom, she did the exact opposite. She walked out and left the door wide open.

Just what I need, Mia thought to herself as she walked back to her cubicle. *New probationers to break in when my caseload is quiet and I have all of my probationers in check.*

"*How'd it go?*" Isabelle asked when Mia sat down at her desk.

"I'll fill you in later," Mia answered as she picked up her tablet, rose, and headed to the waiting room to meet with her first scheduled appointment for the day.

Mia opened the door to the crowded waiting room, and looked into the anxious faces of the men and women who immediately turned their attention toward her, hoping they would not be spending their entire day awaiting the arrival of their probation officer.

Several of the faces looking back at her were familiar. Some of them maintained regular schedules with their officers, and reported faithfully at the same time on the same day of the week.

If there was one thing Mia learned during her years of work as a probation officer, it was this: Crime knows no color, race, age, religion, education, marital status, gender, social status, or sexual orientation. Over the years, Mia and her field partners have made home visits in some of the worst and best neighborhoods in Hampton Roads.

"*Mr. Pinkton? Stanley Pinkton?*"

Stanley Pinkton rose quickly from his seat in the corner of the large room and made his way to the door, where Mia extended her hand and followed him to an interview room a short distance down a lengthy hallway.

"*Good morning, Mr. Pinkton. How have you been doing?*" Mia asked as she took a seat across from him in a steel-colored chair. She placed her tablet on the small desk that separated them.

"*Pretty good, Officer Wells. Can't complain,*" he answered politely.

Stanley Pinkton had been on probation for almost five years following a seven-year sentence for passing bad checks. It was his first conviction in over ten years, and his last since sentencing. At the age of thirty-eight, Stanley was high on Mia's list of probationers she determined would be appropriate for an early discharge.

"Here's the story, Mr. Pinkton. I'm going to drug test you today, and I need you to bring me a copy of your most recent pay stubs and proof of your residence. If you're still drug-free and working, I'm going to apply for an early discharge for you," Mia said.

Stanley's face lit up.

"Are you serious, Officer Wells? You mean I won't have to be on probation anymore?" Stanley asked.

"That is exactly what it means. It's not up to me, though. It's up to the sentencing judge. I'm just going to submit a report, telling the judge of your satisfactory compliance since you have been on probation. If the judge agrees, he or she will discharge you from probation," Mia explained.

"Give me the cup," Stanley said eagerly, his hand outstretched across the table.

Just about every day for two months, Mia delivered the same news to one of her probationers.

At least they're getting a second chance, Mia said to herself.

When will I?

7

On Thursday night, Mia unlocked the front door of the church, turned on the lights, and walked into the sanctuary for choir rehearsal.

She knew the peace and quiet of the room would be lost as soon as the choir members and musicians arrived; but for a moment, she stood quietly before the altar as the single overhead light bathed her in a soft glow.

In the stillness of the moment, she thought about everything that had taken place in her life following her relocation to Virginia from New York three years prior, especially the night fire engulfed her sister Paula's townhouse.

The same night she met Jayson, a chance encounter that exposed a genuine love for another human being Mia never knew she had.

While she stood at the altar, she envisioned standing before Jayson, dressed in the beautiful white wedding dress she purchased, surrounded by smiling family and friends.

In the moment, she could hear her pastor ask, *"Do you, Mia, promise to love Jayson for better or for worse, for richer or for poorer, in sickness and in health, 'til death do you part?"*

Mia answered softly, *"I do."*

Just as quickly, a second vision appeared. Mia saw herself walking up the aisle, arm in arm, with Syrene, and when her pastor asked, *"Who gives this woman to be married to this man?"*

Mia said, *"I do."*

As if God descended from heaven to deliver Mia from a moment of sadness, the door to the sanctuary opened.

It was Reverend Holloway.

"Good evening, Sister Mia," he said. *"Hope I'm not interrupting your quiet moment with the Lord."*

"Good evening, Reverend. Not at all. I was enjoying the peace before my noisy choir members get here. How is everything going with the prison ministry? Have you been in contact with the man I introduced to you at the jail? The one who played drums at the service?" Mia asked.

"As a matter of fact, I have," Reverend Holloway said. *"He requested a clergy visit from me and I met with him Monday. He seems really serious about turning his life around. Of course, I'm not at liberty to discuss his background, but he has quite a testimony. I thought my life was a mess, but he has me beat."*

"You know I know, Reverend. I have been working with criminals for nine years and sometimes I wonder if they can and will ever overcome the behaviors of their past," Mia said.

"It is doable, Sister Mia. Look at me. The Lord changed me. Trust me; if God can change me, there is hope for anyone. Anyway, the good news is that he plans to attend Wayside when he is released. Hopefully, you and the musicians will find room for his gifts," Reverend Holloway added.

"We will, Reverend. He'll be more likely to stay with us if we keep him busy. If you can, let me know when he'll be released," Mia said.

"Will do, Sister Mia. I'm headed to my office. Have a great rehearsal tonight," Reverend Holloway said as Mia walked over and powered the musical equipment.

The doors to the sanctuary opened again. Mia looked up as Daryl Walker casually strolled through, the recessed lights in the ceiling reflecting off his clean-shaven head.

Looking at Daryl, Mia had to recall one of the great hymns of the church...

Savior Lead Me Lest I Stray...

Daryl was one of the first men who introduced himself to her shortly after she joined Wayside. Having just struggled through her breakup with Jayson, she was not ready for a relationship, even for social reasons.

Initially, Daryl continued to pursue her, but after being repeatedly rebuffed, he eventually got the message and moved on.

"Hi Daryl," Mia said as she sat on the organ bench, and turned on the instrument. She bent her head forward until she heard the hum of the Hammond B3 as it sprung to life.

She watched as he strode over to where she was sitting. A year or two younger and much leaner than Mia's extra-large frame, Daryl was a physical therapist. His rich chocolate complexion almost matched hers, with smooth skin and a small dimple in his right cheek. Like Jayson, his teeth were brilliant.

"Good evening, Mia," Daryl said as he leaned down and kissed Mia on her cheek. He had dropped the *"Sister"* title during the chase. She inhaled a whiff of his cologne and almost passed out.

"*Where is everyone?* *Am I early?*" Daryl asked as he parked his handsome self on the front pew.

"*Actually, you're on time. Everyone else seems to be running late. I know one thing, they better get in here. They ought to know me by now. Don't waste my time. If rehearsal is supposed to start at seven-thirty, then I'm starting at seven-thirty. If they're not here by seven-forty-five, I'm going home.*"

"*Good gracious, Mia. You're a tough lady,*" Daryl said.

"*I am not tough,*" Mia said with her hands on her hips. "*I'm just tired of trifling choir members and musicians. When you make a commitment to something or someone, honor it.*"

"*Speaking of commitments, Mia, I was wondering if you would ever entertain making one with me,*" Daryl asked, his muscular arms draped over the back of the chairs.

"*I heard what happened in your last relationship—news kind of travels around here. I thought what you did was incredible,*" Daryl said.

Mia looked at Daryl, but before she could respond, she heard noise in the vestibule and almost instantly, the noise level rose in the sanctuary.

Several choir members ran in, laughing hysterically, as Darlene Walker hobbled in behind them, bending over and dusting something from her clothing.

Georgia could barely talk through her laughter.

"*Sister Mia, Darlene just fell!*" she said.

"*That's not funny, Georgia,*" Darlene stammered. "*I could have really hurt myself.*"

"*She's right, Georgia,*" Mia answered, stifling the urge to laugh herself as Daryl ran over to check on his twin.

"*You don't understand, Sister Mia,*" Georgia explained. "*We keep telling her to wear flat shoes in the parking lot because it's unpaved. But no! Miss Thang wanted to get out of her car and run across the parking lot to the front door in her three-inch heels. She almost made it, too, but lost her footing near the steps and fell forward through the front door. The noise you heard was her landing in the vestibule. I got it all on video, too! I knew she wasn't going to make it!*"

Ouch, Mia thought as the rest of the choir members huddled around Georgia as she replayed the video on her phone of Darlene's humiliating fall through the church's front door.

"*Are you okay, Darlene?*" Mia and Daryl asked as he helped his sister to a nearby pew.

The rest of the choir members and musicians who continued to watch the replay of the video howled with laughter.

"I believe so, Daryl, but I need you to go to the trunk of my car and get my flats. My heel broke," Darlene said as she whimpered over the destruction of her expensive-looking high-heeled right shoe.

"Shouldn't have had them on anyway. Trying to be cute," Georgia taunted, still replaying the video for the latecomers.

"Be nice, Georgia. We all know Darlene. She is who she is," Mia responded. *"And turn that video off, and I better not see it on social media!"*

"Mia's right," Daryl said. *"Darlene has always been a diva, even when we were kids. I'm embarrassed to admit this, but when we were little, she wanted a sister to play with, but it was just the two of us. So, she'd put makeup on me and I used to have to dress up and play princess with her. You just don't know."*

"She had you cross-dressing Daryl?" Georgia asked a little too loudly, temporarily shifting the focus from Darlene to her brother.

"Yes I did," Darlene answered boldly. *"He was the best brother a girl could ever ask for, and he still is,"* Darlene said, while looking directly at Mia.

Georgia and her friends could not take any more. They laughed until tears fell from their eyes.

"Thanks sis. I try," he replied as he leaned down and unbuckled the shoe that still strapped to her left foot.

"Okay, okay. Enough of the family bonding. Go get her flats so we can get rehearsal started please. The rest of you can go straight to the choir stand. And for the last time, Georgia, turn off that video," Mia demanded.

Mia walked over to Darlene.

"Are you okay, really? Maybe you need to go to the emergency room and have your foot X-rayed. It could be fractured or something," Mia asked.

85

"No, that won't be necessary. I'm more embarrassed than anything else. But let me ask you a question, Mia. Why won't you give my brother a chance? He really likes you," Darlene said with a mischievous smile.

"Did it ever occur to you that it's because I can't imagine having someone as dramatic as you as my sister-in-law?" Mia answered jokingly.

Darlene laughed.

"Seriously Mia. He's really a good guy. Give him a chance," she pleaded.

"Get in the choir stand, Darlene," Mia said as she smiled and walked away.

At the conclusion of the rehearsal, Daryl was leaning against a light pole near Mia's car in the church's parking lot.

"Did you really think I was going to let you get away without responding to my question?" Daryl asked.

"What question was that?" Mia replied sheepishly.

"The one about you making a commitment with me," Daryl answered.

Mia thought about Daryl's question and his sister's disclosure.

Maybe I need to give him a chance, Mia pondered. *What do I have to lose?*

"I'll pray about it. How's that?" Mia said.

He smiled and Mia almost melted.

"That'll work for me. In the meantime, may I have your phone number?" he asked.

"Actually, let me have yours. I don't give my number to a man who will not give me his," she said.

Daryl recited the number to Mia, who in turn called the number in his presence. When his phone rang, she said, *"You now have my number."*

"Thank you, Mia, for giving me a chance," Daryl said.

"Thank your sister. She thinks very highly of you," Mia said.

"Does she really?" Daryl inquired.

"As a matter of fact, she does. She's quite the matchmaker," Mia responded as she clicked the remote to her car. Daryl reached over and opened her car door.

"I'm going to have to thank her for putting in a word for me. Get home safe, Mia. I will call you tomorrow," Daryl said, flashing his brilliant smile.

As Mia drove out of the parking lot, she said to herself, *I pray to God I'm not headed into another heartbreaking encounter.*

Almost immediately, Mia heard the still small Voice.

Old things are passed away.

8

Paula removed the blood pressure cuff from the arm of one of the elderly church members after service Sunday morning.

"Your pressure is one-sixty-five over ninety-one, Mother Thompson." Paula said. *"That's pretty high. When was the last time you saw a doctor?"*

Mother Thompson paused and tapped her chubby index finger on her chin.

"I don't remember", she answered.

"Well, I'm going to speak to your son and suggest he schedule an appointment for you as soon as possible. Until then, try to lay off fried and salty foods. Can you do that?" Paula asked.

"Not today, dear. My family always comes to my house for Sunday dinner, and I have to go home and fry chicken. I have a pot of greens on the stove as we speak," Mother Thompson said, licking her lips.

Exasperated, Paula asked, "Where is your son?" as she looked around the fellowship hall. "Never mind. I see him. You wait right here," Paula said as she walked in his direction.

The outside door to the fellowship hall opened and a man walked in, his head slightly lowered as if he was trying to remain unnoticed.

Several of the young women seated at a table close to the door eyed him suspiciously.

"Missed the entire church service, but he's right on time for the refreshments," Caryl said as she shoved a bite-size chicken salad sandwich in her mouth.

"*Be quiet, Caryl,*" Deacon Samuel Grey, head of the Deacon's Ministry sternly said as he walked toward the man. "*We don't know why he's here.*"

"*Good afternoon, sir. May I help you?*" Deacon Sam asked kindly, extending his right hand.

"*Is Reverend Holloway here?*" the man asked, barely raising his head but shaking Deacon Sam's hand.

"*I believe he is. Follow me, sir*", Deacon Sam said.

Deacon Sam led the man past several cloth-covered tables where men and women dressed in medical uniforms performed a variety of physical exams on the participants.

Some of the people were shaking their heads after stepping off scales, while others were undergoing blood pressure screenings.

The young women continued to eye the man as he and Deacon Sam walked across the room. The man never raised his head.

"He looks sketchy," Caryl said, turning up her nose as if something foul was in the air.

"You have a lot of nerve, Caryl. You were high as a kite when you first came to Wayside," Jennifer said as she broke a potato chip in half and popped one into her mouth.

"That ain't right, Jen," Caryl said. *"Don't be bringin' up my past!"*

"Then you of all people need to stop judgin' other folks," Jennifer replied.

Deacon Sam stopped at the third door on the right and knocked.

"Yes?" Reverend Holloway answered.

Deacon Sam opened the door and poked his head inside. *"Reverend Holloway, there's a man here to see you,"* he said.

"Thank you, Deek. I'm just about finished with a call from another member.   Ask him to have a seat please." Reverend Holloway said.

"No problem, Rev," Deacon Sam replied as he closed the door behind him.

"He will be with you in a few moments, sir. Would you like some refreshments? We are in the midst of our monthly health screening," Deacon Sam said.

"Yes sir. I didn't get a chance to eat this morning before I left the ...." The man stopped speaking abruptly.

"Well, you wait right here and I will fix you a plate. We're serving light refreshments so that means we only have sandwiches and cookies. Will that be all right?" Deacon Sam asked.

"Sounds good to me. Thank you, sir," the man said.

Shortly after Deacon Sam headed into the kitchen, Reverend Holloway's office door swung open.

"A man of his word! You said you would come, and here you are," Reverend Holloway said as he grabbed Jackson Braynor's outstretched hand and pulled him into a bear hug.

"I told you I was coming. Sorry I missed the service this morning, but it took them forever to release me. I took the bus straight here," Jackson stated.

"Where are your belongings?" Reverend Holloway asked, looking around.

"I left my bags in the bushes on the side of the church. I didn't want to come in here looking like a homeless person, carrying big black plastic bags," Jackson said.

"I understand. Come on. Let's get you something to eat," Reverend Holloway said as he led Jackson to a table in the fellowship hall.

Their timing was perfect, because Deacon Sam was leaving the kitchen with a plate stacked with food.

"Here you go, sir. Seems like someone fried chicken and they tried to hide it. I sniffed it out and put some on your plate," Deacon Sam said proudly.

"Thank you, sir," Jackson answered as Deacon Sam handed the plate to him.

"You want a plate, Rev?" Deacon Sam asked.

"No thanks, Deek. I'm going to eat when I get home," Reverend Holloway said.

Deacon Sam turned and headed back into the kitchen, while Jackson picked up a chicken leg and took a bite.

Wiping his mouth with a napkin, Jackson looked around and asked, *"Is Sister Mia still here? I was hoping to see her about playing in the band here at the church."*

Reverend Holloway scanned the crowd.

"I don't see her, but her sister is right over there," Reverend Holloway said while pointing in Paula's direction.

"Sister Paula?" Reverend Holloway called.

Paula turned her head slightly, but resumed taking a man's blood pressure.

"Sister Paula. Over here," Reverend Holloway repeated, this time waving.

Paula smiled and motioned for him to give her a minute. After saying a few words to her patient, she turned and headed in Reverend Holloway's direction.

"Hi Reverend Holloway. Do you need something?" Paula asked, removing her latex gloves.

"Yes, Paula. This is Jackson Braynor. He's a drummer who is interested in playing at our church. He was hoping to catch your sister before she left," Reverend Holloway said.

"Oh. She left already. But anyway, hello, Jackson, and welcome to Wayside," Paula said as she smiled, extending her hand.

"Thank you. Nice meeting you, Sister Paula. Do you know what night the choir rehearses?" Jackson asked.

"Rehearsals are usually on Thursday nights, but there won't be any for the next two weeks. There is revival service every night this week, and the following week the choir has to go out with Elder Rhodes. He has a preaching engagement at Mercy Seat Baptist Church on Todds Lane in Hampton," Paula said.

Trying to mask his disappointment, Jackson said, *"May I leave a phone number with you so you can give it to your sister? I'd really like to speak with her about playing here."*

"Sure, just leave it with Reverend Holloway and I will see that my sister gets the message. Good meeting you," Paula said as she walked off and returned to her patients.

Reverend Holloway turned to Jackson.

"So, what's your plan? Where are you headed when you leave here?" he asked.

Jackson finished chewing a piece of bread before he replied.

"I'm going to my brother's place here in Hampton. He said I can stay with him until I get my own apartment. I'm hoping it will be soon, because I know how he's living, and if I stay around that element, it'll only be a matter of time before I'll be back in jail."

"You're a smart man," Reverend Holloway said. "For your information, we have several members here at Wayside who rent rooms and apartments. Once you get a job, I'll make a few calls for you so we can get you settled in a better environment."

"They won't mind having someone with a criminal record living in their apartments?" Jackson asked.

"Not at all. That's how we are here at Wayside. We minister to real people with real issues," Reverend Holloway said.

"I'm glad to hear that," Jackson said as he rose to dump his empty paper plate in the nearest garbage container.

"I'm going to give you a ride to your brother's apartment," Reverend Holloway said as he rose from the table. "Wait here while I go back to my office and get my things."

"Thanks Rev. I'm really glad I met you at that service at the jail. I believe it was a divine appointment," Jackson said.

"It was, Jackson. God is always up to something," Reverend Holloway said.

As Reverend Holloway headed to his office, Jackson watched the flurry of activity that was going on in the fellowship hall.

The health care ministry was packing up their equipment and sanitizing the tabletops and seats. The culinary ministry was clearing the tables and inviting people to the kitchen to take the leftover food home.

Jackson noticed that the young women who had been sitting at the table by the door were not sitting there to be social. They were waiting for the announcement that there were leftovers!

He watched as they practically tripped over each other on their way to the food table, grabbed white Styrofoam containers, stuffed them with sandwiches and cookies, and then rushed out of a side door without even saying goodbye to each other.

So much for Christian fellowship, Jackson laughed to himself.

A short time later, Jackson heard a voice behind him.

"I'm ready Jackson. Now where did you leave your belongings?" Reverend Holloway asked.

"My bags are on the right side of the building, in the bushes," Jackson said.

"Okay. Let me walk over and give your contact information to Paula so she can give it to her sister. Then, I'll go get my car and drive over to meet you. I don't want you to have to carry your bags while people are still mingling in the parking lot," Reverend Holloway said.

"That's very thoughtful of you, Reverend Holloway. I appreciate it," Jackson said.

"Like I told you before, I've been there. I've felt the shame and the embarrassment. We're here to help you get the life

back you surrendered to the streets years ago," Reverend Holloway said. *"As far as we are concerned here at Wayside, it doesn't matter what you've done in the past, once you've given your life to the Lord Jesus, old things are passed away."*

9

Paula unlocked the front door of her new townhouse after driving from the church and immediately inhaled the aroma of her roast simmering in the slow cooker.

Of course, Mia had not touched a thing in the kitchen. Instead, she was unpacking boxes and arranging china in the hutch in the dining area.

"You couldn't even cook the rice, Mia?" Paula asked, looking at her brand new gleaming stovetop.

"You know I can't cook, Paula. Why would you even ask?" Mia responded.

"How were you on your way up the aisle in a wedding dress and you can't even cook a pot of rice?" Paula asked.

"We were going to be eating out a lot," Mia joked. "Cooking ain't my calling. I'll stick to the music ministry; you handle the culinary and the health ministry."

Paula laughed as she walked into her master bedroom suite. She undressed quickly and returned to the kitchen in jeans and a tee shirt.

"Boy, am I glad to get out of those clothes," Paula said. "It's bad enough I have to wear a uniform to work. Having to wear it to church was painful. However, we had a good turnout for the health screening event."

"Oh, by the way," Paula continued, reaching into her purse for the drummer's contact information. "A man named Jackson showed up at the church looking for you. He was hoping to meet up with you about playing in the band."

"Wow, he made it after all. I'm surprised," Mia remarked as she gently placed a saucer in the china cabinet.

"Where do you know him from?" Paula asked as she handed Mia his information. "Did he play at Unity?"

Remembering her promise of confidentiality, Mia replied, "No. We had an outside engagement and we didn't have a drummer. He offered to play for us. He was really good, so I told him if he ever needed a job as a drummer to let me know."

"Well, he was sure disappointed that he missed you today. Hopefully, you'll be able to contact him and he can play at our church. I always get excited when I see men who want to work in the church. They are so rare," Paula said.

"Yes they are, especially the serious and committed ones. They are as rare as pearls. Sadly, these days, so many church musicians aren't committed to ministry; they're just in it for the money. As a result, it's hard for churches to keep faithful musicians because there's always another church somewhere willing to offer them more money," Mia said.

"You don't seem to suffer from that problem. You've always been surrounded by talented and faithful musicians," Paula said.

"The Bible says we reap what we have sown. I've sown faithful service into all the ministries I've served; so I'm reaping it back," Mia said with a smile.

"I hope everything works out for him. He seems like a decent man," Paula said.

That's what you think, Mia said under her breath.

"Well, I'll give him a call and see when we can begin rehearsing with him," Mia said as she put the paper bearing his phone number in her purse.

Changing the subject, Mia asked, "How much longer do I have to wait for this roast to be done?" as she lifted the cover from the slow cooker and inspected her dinner.

"It's ready now. The problem is there's no side dish to go with it, thanks to you," Paula said with a laugh.

"*Don't you have bread?*" Mia asked, walking over to a cabinet and poking her head inside.

"*For someone of your class and education, you can be so tacky sometimes,*" Paula said.

"*Whatever. Slice up that roast, give me two slices of bread and as they say in church, 'I'll be out of your way'.*" Mia said as she pointed her index finger toward the ceiling.

As they sat at Paula's kitchen island, eating, Mia said, "*Did I tell you that Daryl Walker asked me out last week?*"

"*No, you did not! You told me he was interested before; he's still on the prowl?*" Paula asked.

"*Apparently he is. He arrived at rehearsal last Thursday before everyone else, and we talked for a few minutes. After rehearsal, he was waiting by my car, and asked if he could have my number. He promised to call the following day, and to my surprise, he actually did,*" Mia said.

"Really?" Paula said excitedly. *"What did you two talk about?"*

"The conversation was pretty general. We talked about our work and the things we enjoy doing with our free time, the little we both have," Mia said.

Mia rose from her seat, opened the refrigerator, and poured herself a glass of ginger ale.

Leaning against the granite countertop, Mia asked her sister, *"What do you think, Paula? He's a couple of years younger than I am, but I don't really care about that. I'm just not sure how serious he is. I don't have time for games."*

"The only way you will get to know him is by spending time with him, Mia. He doesn't seem to be a player; I've never even seen him with another woman. Truthfully, I was starting to wonder if he was gay," Paula said.

Mia laughed. *"Why did you have to go there, Paula? Honestly, I haven't seen him with anyone, either, including his own sister Darlene."*

"Can you blame him, Mia? He would probably be in jail on an assault charge by now, fighting off all the men Darlene attracts like flies," Paula said.

Mia laughed again as she returned to her seat at the island.

"You're right, Paula. Even when we were at the jail and Darlene was huddled in a corner with an inmate, I would have thought Daryl might have stepped in, but he was nowhere to be found. I think he stays clear of her on purpose. He has a good career and therefore can't afford to be caught up with his sister's shenanigans," Mia said.

"I don't know, Paula," Mia continued as she ate the rest of the food on her plate. *"I'm kind of apprehensive about entering another relationship."*

"Don't be," Paula said. "It's about that time for both of us. I'm ready to start dating myself. It's been years for me."

Mia turned and eyed her younger sister questionably.

"Oh really? Anybody I know?" Mia asked.

"Not at all," Paula said. "I just think I'm ready to enjoy the company of a man."

She rose from her seat, collected her plate and flatware, and headed for the sink to rinse them before placing them in the dishwasher.

"It's been years, Mia. It's time I got over my fear of dating. I can't expect every man I meet to be as heartless and abusive as the last man I dated," Paula said.

Yes, it had been years, Mia recalled.

Mia remembered what happened the last time Paula seriously dated. She was sexually assaulted by her so-called "date", and later dropped off at an unfamiliar subway station in Brooklyn, NY to find her way home.

Since then, although Paula would go out with men socially, she had not been in a serious relationship.

"Well, I don't have to tell you to be careful," Mia said. *"There are a lot of men out there who claim they are looking for a good woman, but don't know how to treat one when they find one. They're all dogs if you ask me! I was fortunate to find Jayson, but I doubt very seriously if there is another man as wonderful as he is. That's why I'm a little skeptical about getting involved with Daryl Walker."*

"I guess we'll both have to step out on faith, Mia. We need to let go of the failures of the past and give men a chance," Paula said. *"Especially saved men."*

Paula heard a Voice from heaven.

That's right, Paula.

Old things are passed away.

10

Reverend Holloway concentrated on the road before him as Jackson spoke on the phone with his brother.

"Hey, Roland. I'm on my way to your house. Anybody home?" Jackson asked.

"Yeah, Michelle is there. La'Nae turned three-years-old today, so we're throwin' a birthday party for her," Roland said.

"My niece is three already? That went by quick. Wait a minute? You're not at the party?" Jackson asked.

"No, Bro. I had to leave to take care of some business," Roland said. *"I'll be back in a few, though. Just make yourself comfortable 'til I get there."*

"*Will do. Thanks again for letting me stay with you guys,*" Jackson said.

"*Never a problem, Bro. We're family,*" Roland said before hanging up.

Jackson disconnected the call and handed the phone back to Reverend Holloway.

"*Thanks, Rev for letting me use your phone,*" Jackson said.

"*No problem, Jackson. I understand the challenges you face. I've been through it myself, having to regroup after being incarcerated. The good news is, this time you have help,*" Reverend Holloway said.

Jackson looked out the window. "*At the next light, make a left,*" he said.

The neighborhood was definitely not an ideal location for someone trying to stay away from trouble. Litter lined the streets, as did young men and women hanging out in front of the numerous boarded up stores on the block, as if they were awaiting the arrival of a parade.

For a lazy Sunday afternoon, there was a lot of activity going on.

"I haven't been on this part of town in a while. Looks like a lot of ministry needs to be happening here,' Reverend Holloway said.

"You'd think with all of the churches in this city, everybody in the neighborhood would be saved," Jackson said.

"It should be the case, but most of the folks who attend churches in this neighborhood are probably afraid of these people and walk right by them without speaking," Reverend Holloway said.

They approached a duplex apartment complex.

"This is it, Reverend," Jackson said, pointing to Building #203.

Reverend Holloway eased his car into the first available space, careful to avoid driving over fragments of broken beer bottles in parking lot.

After putting the car in park, Reverend Holloway pressed a button on his driver's side door, and the trunk popped open.

Jackson slowly got out of the car, stretched, and took in the sights and breathed in the aroma of his brother's neighborhood.

Someone nearby was smoking weed.

I can tell already that this is not the place for me, he thought to himself.

"Thanks again for the ride, Rev, and all you've done for me. I'll see you this week at the revival, whether Sister Mia calls me or not," Jackson said.

"She'll call, Jackson. I'm sure of it. Sister Mia is serious about music ministry, and when she extended the offer for

you to come to Wayside, she meant it. She's going to make room for you in the band," Reverend Holloway said as he handed Jackson his bags from the trunk of the car.

Jackson smiled and said, *"I'm glad because I need to get back involved in the church. There's nothing out here in the streets."*

"You got that right, son. As you can see by looking around at the people in this neighborhood, a lot of men your age haven't figured that out yet. And unfortunately, by the time they do, they'll be sitting behind bars, just like we were," Reverend Holloway said.

Jackson quickly surveyed his brother's *"busy"* neighborhood. His eyes scanned the people congregated on the street or in the parking lot. His nose inhaled the lingering smell of marijuana in the air. His ears recalled the words of his brother, Roland; *"I had to leave to take care of some business."*

He turned and faced Reverend Holloway.

"I know you hear it all the time, Rev, but I'm dead serious. This isn't the life for me anymore. I don't care what I have to do or where I have to go, the one place I'm not going is back to jail," Jackson declared.

Reverend Holloway eyed Jackson Braynor. He was standing on the curb, clad in black jeans and a *Steelers* tee shirt. Both hands were grasping the twisted red handles of black plastic trash bags that probably contained his worldly goods.

Gone was the slump. It had been replaced with the posture of a man determined to elevate himself above his past acts and present circumstances.

He's not playing this time, Reverend Holloway noted.

"I stand in agreement with you, Jackson. You're not going back to jail," Reverend Holloway said.

Jackson smiled, shook Reverend Holloway's outstretched hand, and said, *"Thank you for believing in me, Rev. I'll* contact you sometime tomorrow after I check in with my probation officer."

"I look forward to hearing from you. Be safe out here," Reverend Holloway said as he walked around to the driver's side of his car and opened the door.

"I will. I'm not coming back out until tomorrow," Jackson replied.

Wise move, Reverend Holloway thought as he surveyed Jackson's surroundings one last time before getting into his car. He'll be back in jail within a week if he doesn't get out of this neighborhood.

"Remember, Jackson. There is new life ahead of you. Old things are passed away," Reverend Holloway said through the open passenger window as he backed out of the parking space.

Jackson turned and walked toward his brother's apartment building. From the sidewalk, he could hear the voices of children laughing, R&B music playing, and adults gossiping.

The door to his brother's apartment was slightly open when he approached. He knocked twice on the doorsill, but the music overwhelmed his attempt to announce his arrival.

He pushed the door in and walked into complete pandemonium.

The few adults in the room were sitting on a sofa by the open window. Folding chairs were arranged around the carpeted living room. A magician with an off-white rabbit fascinated several of the children, but the rest were all over the place, running with balloons in their hands and lollipops in their mouths.

Roland's wife, Michelle, saw Jackson first as he weaved a path from the front door to the kitchen.

"Hi Jackson," she said, wiping her hands on a paper towel before giving him a hug.

"Roland called and said you were on your way. Good to see you. I guess you can just drop your things in our bedroom upstairs and sit up there if you want, unless you're in the mood for all of this chaos," she yelled over the loud music.

"Actually, I think I'll just drop my bags in the bedroom and sit on the porch for a while. I just came out of a chaotic environment; the only difference was the chaos was created by adults acting like children," Jackson said jokingly.

"I understand, Jackson. It is a bit much in here today," Michelle said, shaking her head. "I can't blame Roland for leaving. If I could get out of here, I would."

"What time is the party supposed to be over?" Jackson asked.

"Six o'clock. But some of these kids will probably be here longer because their parents dropped them off and are *somewhere shopping in the mall or getting their nails done,"* Michelle answered.

Looks like I won't be getting much rest tonight, Jackson thought to himself

After conversing with Michelle for several more minutes, Jackson left the kitchen and headed upstairs in the direction of their bedroom. Although Roland and Michelle lived in a less-than-desirable apartment complex, they always kept their apartment immaculate. Their bedroom was stylishly decorated with solid oak furniture and bright gold and navy blue curtains.

Jackson dropped his bags in a corner of the room, walked downstairs, through the noisy living room, and out the front door, closing it behind him.

Finding a chair on the small porch, Jackson sat down and observed a group of people hanging out in the parking lot.

So many people with nothing to do and nowhere to go.

From somewhere to his left, Jackson heard an all-too-familiar, booming voice.

"Yo Jack! Is dat you? When did you get out?"

Dang. Of all the people! Smokey! Why don't you just tell the town? Jackson said to himself.

He watched as one of his eldest cousins, Preston, aka *"Smokey"* Braynor made his way up the stairs to the porch where Jackson was sitting.

There was a reason Preston was known as *"Smokey,"* and it wasn't because he sounded or looked anything like the famous singer.

Smokey parked his narrow backside on the top step, pulled out a pack of cigarettes, and lit one.

Wisps of white smoke floated through Smokey's thin fingers, several bearing what Jackson knew to be decades-old marijuana stains.

"So, when did you git out, Jack?" Smokey asked as he peered over his dark sunglasses, which were totally unnecessary considering the dreariness of the afternoon.

"Earlier this morning, Smokey. I'm staying with Roland for a few days until I get my own place. I can't stay around here. There's too much going on," Jackson said.

"Yeah, itz kinda busy 'round here, but I like it like dis. Good for bizness, ya know," Smokey said with his toothless grin, tapping his left jacket pocket.

"Can I hook you up with a lil' somethin', Jack? It'll be on the house. Kinda a 'welcome home' gift," Smokey asked.

"No thanks, Smokey. I'm clean now and I plan to stay that way," Jackson said as he rose from his chair, about to head back indoors.

"Dat's what we all say when we git out," Smokey mocked.

"Well, I jus' want you to know I'm here for you, jus' in case you need me. Good seein' ya! Welcome home, Cuz,"

124

Smokey said as he extended his right hand toward Jackson.

Jackson reached down to shake his outstretched hand, and realized too late that Smokey's hand was not empty.

Jackson felt the tiny plastic bag against the palm of his right hand at the same moment he heard the undercover officer shout, *"Put your hands behind your back!"*

I don't believe this, Jackson said in disgust as he complied with the officer's commands.

A single tear streamed down his cheek.

What am I going to say to Reverend Holloway? I just told him less than an hour ago that I was not going back to jail. Will he believe this wasn't my fault, or will he—like my father—give up on me? Jackson said to himself as he was escorted to a police car, bound for the city jail.

11

Mia was walking in the door of her apartment when her cell phone rang.

She fumbled through her purse, found her phone, and answered right before the call went to her voice mail.

"Hello?"

"Good evening, Mia." She recognized the smooth voice immediately. It was Reverend Holloway.

Usually happy, his voice bore the tone of disappointment.

"I just received a collect call from Jackson Braynor. He's at the city jail. Unfortunately, he was arrested this afternoon on a misdemeanor drug possession charge," he said.

Mia could not contain her laughter.

"Wait a minute, Rev. Didn't he just get out this morning? How did he manage to get arrested less than eight hours after his release? Is he that stupid?"

"Sister Mia," Reverend Holloway said, *"Before we begin to pass judgment on him, don't you think we need to find out all of the facts?   After all, even the United States Constitution says we are innocent until proven guilty."*

"I suppose we should, but in my professional opinion, I already know where he is going: Back before the sentencing judge and back to the county jail! He's on probation, isn't he? Why in the world would he possess drugs on his first day out of jail, knowing that his probation officer is going to drug test him at his first appointment tomorrow? For someone who claimed he wasn't going back to jail, he certainly did everything he could to make sure he would end up there, now didn't he?" Mia asked as she walked into her living room and sat on the sofa.

Reverend Holloway could offer no rebuttal. From the moment he left Jackson on the curb in front of his brother's apartment complex, he knew Jackson's chances of survival in that neighborhood were slim.

It was not the environment for someone trying to get his or her life together. Yet, he held out hope that Jackson would somehow endure; unfortunately, for Jackson, it didn't happen.

Nevertheless, I made a promise to him I plan to keep. I told him I would help him, and if he reaches out to me, I will keep my promise. Every time I fell, someone was there to pick me up. I must do the same for him, Reverend Holloway said to himself.

"Sister Mia, if Jackson reaches out to me, I will continue to work with him through the prison ministry, and when he is released, I hope his position as a drummer in the church's band will be waiting for him as well," Reverend Holloway said.

"No doubt, Reverend Holloway," Mia said. *"His current legal situation has no bearing on his ministry gifts. I just hope when he gets out next time he'll finally give up the street life once and for all. Enough is enough."*

"I agree. Thank you, Sister Mia. Have a good night and I will see you this week at the revival service," Reverend Holloway said before ending the call.

Mia felt the urge to share the news with Paula but thought otherwise. Not one to gossip or as the Christian Covenant discouraged *"needlessly exposing the infirmities of others,"* Mia instead rose from the sofa and headed to her bedroom to prepare for her upcoming work week.

I wonder what kind of mood Stacey is going to be in this week? Mia pondered.

Mia's immediate supervisor, Stacey Abraham, was a workaholic, so Mia could never look forward to a reprieve from her by way of personal leave, vacation leave, or sick leave. The only breaks from Stacey that Mia enjoyed took place when the office was closed on weekends and national holidays.

Stacey probably wouldn't even take bereavement leave if someone in her immediate family died. She'd come in before the funeral and come back to work as soon as the minister said, "Ashes to ashes, dust to dust", Mia thought to herself.

She really needs a life.

After picking out her outfit for the following day, Mia walked into her bathroom and turned on the shower.

She never bothered wearing a shower cap; there was no point. Most of her hair would be sticking out of the sides, anyway.

She stepped in, applied scented shower gel to a sponge, and allowed the warm soapy water to stream down her chocolate face to her pedicured feet.

She thought about Daryl Walker.

Maybe I shouldn't be thinking about him while I'm naked in this shower, she thought to herself.

"I'm sorry God. I repent!!!" Mia prayed, her eyes turned upward.

To help stay focused, she started singing that great hymn of the church...

"Jesus keep me near the cross..."

Mia stepped out of the shower, grabbed a plush bath towel off the rack, and began the process of drying herself. She then applied deodorant, her favorite lotion over her flawless skin, put on her pajamas, brushed her teeth, and slipped in between the cool sheets of her queen-sized bed.

She briefly entertained the thought of calling Daryl but changed her mind.

What if he is entertaining someone else? I'll be so embarrassed, Mia thought to herself.

As if he was reading her mind, her cell phone rang.

"Good evening, Mia," Daryl's smooth tenor voice floated over the line.

Trying desperately to sound nonchalant but knowing she was failing miserably, Mia responded, *"Hi Daryl. How are you doing? I'm surprised to hear from you."*

"Surprised? I'm not sure why you would be surprised Mia. I told you before rehearsal last Thursday and during our phone conversation the following evening that I want to be seriously involved with you. This is not a game to me, Mia. I'm not looking for a fling. I'm too old for games. Unless for some reason you're not ready, I'm ready for a committed relationship."

Mia was taken aback by the boldness of his statement. It was obvious Daryl was serious. Perhaps the time had arrived for Mia to finally let go of *"what was."*

Mia's former fiancé, Jayson, was happily married to Syrene.

It was time for Mia to move on.

Daryl Walker seemed like a suitable mate for Mia. He was saved, attractive, educated, and owned his own business. Yes, he was a bit younger, but he proved himself a mature gentleman.

There appeared to be no reason why Mia should turn down his offer for a serious relationship.

Mia took a deep breath. She exhaled.

"Daryl, I would like to think I'm ready for a committed relationship again, but I'm not sure. What I am sure of is this: I enjoy talking to you, and I'm sure I will enjoy getting to know you. So, if you don't mind taking it slow, I'm ready to try," Mia said.

"*Best news I heard all day,*" Daryl said. "*I don't mind taking it slow, as long as you'll give us a chance, Mia. I'll call you tomorrow.*"

"*Have a good night, Daryl,*" Mia said with a smile as she disconnected the call and placed her cell phone back on the charger.

She turned off the light and rested her head against her down-filled pillow. As she closed her eyes, she had a vision.

Jayson was standing before her. Even after all the time that had passed since she last saw him, she remembered every detail of his face.

Only this time, he was standing before her as he first stood before her.

As a person she could trust.

On the night of the fire at Paula's townhouse.

Carrying the purse she had left in her seat at the jazz concert earlier that evening.

In her vision, Jayson did not say a word.

Rather, he smiled, turned, and walked away.

Mia opened her eyes.

She received the message he was sent to deliver.

Old things are passed away.

She rolled over onto her side and fell asleep.

12

Mia was sitting at her desk, making phone calls, and clearing up paperwork for the rest of the week.

Overnight, she had caught a very bad cold, but decided to show up and cancel appointments for the week so her co-workers would not get stuck with her workload.

"Wells, get in here!" Stacey Abrams bellowed from her office.

Annoyed, Mia left her cubicle and walked into her supervisor's office.

Stacey never looked up. Instead, she commanded, *"Close the door and sit down."*

Before Stacey could say another word, Mia exploded.

"Stacey, of all of the thoughtless things you could conjure up, finding work for me to do today is the worst! You know I don't feel well and the only reason why I came in today was to clear my schedule for the rest of the week so my co-workers won't have to see the probationers I scheduled appointments with this week. What in the world is so important?"

Stacey looked up from the pile of papers on her desk. For the first time since she saw her supervisor in the elevator over three years prior, Mia noticed the color of Stacey's eyes. They were a bluish-green hue, almost the color of an emerald.

Surprisingly, Stacey didn't react at all to Mia's angry outburst.

Instead, Stacey said, *"I'm kind of embarrassed to ask this of you, but I've been invited out on a date this weekend by a lawyer who works in the district attorney's office. I looked through my closet last night, and I realized I don't have anything appropriate to wear, so since you offered to* take me shopping, I thought maybe you could sit with me before you leave and help me pick out an outfit online."

The anger that had twisted Mia's face immediately turned into delight.

"Are you kidding me? I've been waiting for this day since I got hired! Stacey, I'm gonna hook you up!" Mia said excitedly as she moved toward Stacey's desk.

Stacey suddenly stood with her arms extended in front of her.

"Hold it, hold it," Stacey commanded.

Mia stopped abruptly, confused. "I thought you wanted me to help you?"

"I do, but I'm not stupid," Stacey answered as she reached in her desk drawer and pulled out a mask, latex gloves, and a can of disinfectant.

"You and your germs are not messin' up my hot date this weekend," Stacey said as she donned the mask and gloves and started spraying disinfectant in Mia's direction.

"Oh no you're not!" Mia said with a laugh.

"Oh yes I am!" Stacey answered. *"Now you can sit down at my desk. Make me look fabulous, Wells!"*

"No problem, Stacey. When I get done dressing you, your date won't recognize you when he picks you up!" Mia said as she sat in Stacey's chair.

"Are we doing hair and makeup, too, Stacey?" Mia asked, her eyes scanning various clothing sites on the computer screen.

"Don't push it, Wells," Stacey said.

"Alright, alright, boss," Mia said. *"All I know is I better get an invite to the wedding when this is all over."*

"Now you're really pushing it, Wells," Stacey said with a chuckle.

13

Jackson reached over to signal for the bus driver to stop at the next corner. He grabbed the black garbage bag that was on the seat next to him, stood, and walked to the back door.

When the doors opened, he descended the three steps, and found himself on the same pavement he stepped on four months prior. However, this time, he was not headed to his brother's apartment. He learned his lesson; he would stay in a homeless shelter before he jeopardized his freedom again.

Reverend Holloway was in his office when Jackson tapped lightly on his door.

"Hello Brother Jackson. Welcome back," he said, rising from his office chair and embracing him.

"Thanks, Rev", Jackson replied. "I appreciate all you did to get me an early release. I didn't expect you to believe me when I told you I was innocent."

"In all honesty, Jackson, your story was incredible. I mean, what was the likelihood of you getting caught by an undercover cop at the time your cousin pressed a bag of weed into your hand by surprise? Teddy Pendergrass sang a song back in the day entitled 'Bad Luck'. Man, on the day you got out of jail last time, that song should have been your national anthem!" Reverend Holloway said.

They both laughed as Jackson dropped the black garbage bag in a corner and deposited his tall, lean body in an overstuffed chair in Reverend Holloway's spacious office.

Reverend Holloway shuffled several papers around on his desk, and after a few minutes gave Jackson Braynor his undivided attention.

"So, you're headed to a shelter this time? Are you sure that's a good idea?" Reverend Holloway asked with concern.

"Not really, Rev. I'd rather be in my own apartment, but I don't have it like that right now. But I know now I don't need to be anywhere near my brother Roland's apartment. His neighborhood is not the place for me. I learned that the hard way," Jackson said, shaking his head as he continued.

"I can't believe what happened to me, Rev. One minute I was sitting on the porch, minding my own business, and the next minute I thought I was dreaming when the cop was putting those cuffs on me. I could've choked my cousin Smokey for being so stupid. I was so angry at him for doing what he did," Jackson said, his face beginning to burn with anger.

"It happens all the time, Jackson. More often than people realize. All it takes is one foolish person in the crowd, in the car, or in the apartment and everyone's life can be changed for the worse," Reverend Holloway said.

143

"I'm going to guess your cousin Smokey has been in and out of jail most of his life," Reverend Holloway added. "The street life is probably all he knows. It's a shame, but unless he finds the Lord, he'll probably die in the streets or in jail."

"You're right, Rev. Smokey oughta know better. He's almost fifty years old," Jackson said with a sigh.

"That's sad, Jackson. It really is. It's not just the old heads, either. Sister Mia is a federal parole officer, and every month she talks to the young people here at the church and warns them about their friends and associates. I don't know if they're even paying attention. You know these young people. You can't tell them anything; they swear they know it all. Plus, while she's talking, most of them are on their phones, either texting or posting messages on social media. I just hope they start paying attention to the people in their circle because like I said, all it takes is one wrong move—being in the wrong place with the wrong people—to change their lives forever," Reverend Holloway said.

"Don't I know it", Jackson said.

Reverend Holloway sat quietly in deep thought for about thirty seconds. He pushed his chair away from his desk, rose, and walked to his office window.

It was a weekday, so, except for his car, the church's parking lot was empty. However, Reverend Holloway's mind was not.

He stood at the window; his eyes were closed but his ears were open. He turned from the window, sat at his desk, and looked at Jackson for another few moments.

"Jackson, while I was standing by the window, the Lord spoke to me. There's a small apartment in the basement of my house. I'm going to rent it to you. I know you don't have any money right now, so you can do some work around the house in exchange for your rent until you get a job. How does that sound?"

The first of several tears began their descent down Jackson's grateful face.

I can't remember the last time anybody's been this kind to me, Jackson thought as he wiped his eyes with the back of his hands.

"Rev, I don't know how to thank you for your kindness. I'd be honored to stay in your basement apartment. I'm pretty handy, too. I learned carpentry at the jail," Jackson said.

"That's good to know, Jackson. The house is old and needs some work," Reverend Holloway replied.

Reverend Holloway reached for Jackson's bag that was stashed in the corner of his office.

"Come on, let's get out of here," he said.

Jackson rose from his chair, and hugged Reverend Holloway.

"Thanks, Rev. I mean it. I believe this is the break I need," Jackson said.

"I believe so, too, Jackson," Reverend Holloway concurred as Jackson released his embrace and reached for his bag.

"Sometimes that's all it takes. One life-changing turn of events. This very well may be yours, Jackson. If it is, don't blow it," Reverend Holloway said.

Looking him directly in the eye, Jackson said, "I won't blow it, Rev."

After they arrived at Reverend Holloway's house, Jackson settled into the furnished apartment. As predicted, positive things began to occur in his life.

Within a week, Jackson was able to secure a part-time job as a cook at a restaurant in Hampton. Unfortunately, the restaurant served breakfast on Sunday mornings, which made it impossible for Jackson to attend church services.

However, Reverend Holloway understood, and during the week, he and Jackson would spend time studying the Bible and talking about the goodness of the Lord.

Although Jackson could not attend formal church services at Wayside, he was being spiritually fed by Reverend Holloway on a regular basis. When he was not at work, Jackson kept to himself in his little basement apartment, reading the Bible or watching sporting events on television.

He tried reaching out to his father, but after several attempts with no response, Jackson gave up.

For the first time in years, Jackson's life was coming together.

One evening, Jackson sat on the sofa in his small living room, took out a notebook, and began to jot down his short and long-term goals. Satisfied with his list, he closed the notebook, and placed it in the drawer of the end table for safekeeping.

I can and will do this, Jackson declared to himself.

I'm a new creation in Christ.

Old things are passed away.

14

Paula stared hopelessly at the mounting pile of clothes on top of her bed.

I'll never pull an outfit together for my date tonight, she moaned.

It had been years since she had been out on a real date. She had plenty of male friends with whom she would hang out on occasion, going to social events and concerts, but tonight was different.

There was something special going on, and she wanted to make sure her outfit reflected it.

Their friendship began after service one Sunday when he approached her table to get his blood pressure checked.

She could look at him and tell he probably didn't have blood pressure issues. He was tall, thin, and appeared to be in excellent physical condition.

She was correct in her initial assessment. His blood pressure was excellent; one-ten over seventy. He later admitted using the opportunity to ask for her phone number.

Generally reserved, Paula smiled and gave it to him. They have been talking every day for the past three weeks.

He was a very polite man. During their frequent phone conversations, Paula learned he had two jobs. He worked at the YMCA during the week, and as a cook at a restaurant on the weekends. Additionally, he attended classes at the local community college at night, with the goal of becoming a physical education teacher.

He was equally impressed with Paula's academic achievements in nursing school.

"So, what's a fine woman like you doing by yourself?" he asked over the phone one evening.

Paula shared several of her horror stories with him, who found it difficult to contain his anger after hearing of the manner in which some of his fellow brothers treated her.

"I'm so sorry you were treated that way, Paula," he said. *"I promise to make it up to you. I'll never treat you unkindly. Never. You have my word. I wasn't raised like that. My parents have been married for over forty years, and not one time did I see my father mistreat my mother. I believe Godly women are gifts from God. You are a gift, and I will treat you like one."*

Paula was glad she was home alone and he could not see the tears trickling from her eyes.

No man had ever said anything so beautiful to her.

He really seems like a genuine, caring man. I hope I'm not wrong about him, Paula said to herself.

She heard the still small Voice.

Old things are passed away. Behold. All things are become new.

As Paula's thoughts returned to the present, she realized she had yet to tell Mia about her evolving relationship.

I'm a grown, independent, and self-sufficient woman, Paula reminded herself in her bathroom mirror as she carefully applied makeup to her already attractive face.

I don't need Mia's counseling, coaching, correcting, or rescuing anymore. I can handle my own affairs, Paula said with determination, as she eyed herself in the mirror and returned to her master bedroom to make a final decision on which outfit to wear that evening.

Paula chose a purple linen dress with mid-heeled black sandals. She selected a black shawl in case the weather turned chilly.

Just as Paula was about to pull the dress over her braided hair, her cell phone rang.

She looked at the caller ID.

It was Mia.

Goodness, Paula muttered aloud.

She hated lying to her sister, but she really did not want Mia in her personal business anymore.

I have just the solution for that, Paula smiled to herself.

Paula let the call go to her voice mail, finished dressing, and walked out the front door.

15

Mia let the phone ring until it went into Paula's voice mail.

Where is she? Mia wondered. *She should be home by now.*

Mia looked at her watch. It was six-fifty-five p.m.

She began pacing around her living room like a leopard as she had the tendency of doing when something troubled her.

Why am I so upset? Paula is a grown woman, Mia thought as she continued to walk in circles, pausing only to pick up and flip through magazines in which she had no interest.

She tried Paula's number a second time. Again, it went straight to her voice mail.

I know she sees my number on her caller ID. Why isn't she answering my calls? Mia said to herself, angrily.

Mia sat on her sofa and attempted to rationalize her sister's unusual behavior.

Maybe she's taking a nap. That's it. She didn't hear the phone. Or maybe she's in the shower. Maybe she had to work an extra shift at the hospital; her phone would have to be off.

Satisfied with her answers, Mia rose from the sofa, went into the kitchen, and reached for the handle of the refrigerator door.

Her doorbell rang.

Who in the world is it? I didn't invite anyone over here. Oh, maybe it's Paula, Mia said aloud, her mood brightening she anxiously headed toward the door.

He was standing in the rain.

Drops trickled from the top of his umbrella onto his black leather shoes. In his right hand was a bouquet of assorted flowers.

"Are you going to leave me out here all evening or are you going to invite me inside?" he asked.

"What are you doing here, Daryl?" Mia asked as she stepped aside, allowing him to duck into her foyer.

He shook his wet umbrella onto the mat outside the door, and closed it behind himself.

"What do you mean, Mia? I told you I was taking you out to dinner tonight. You forgot?" Daryl asked.

Good Lord, Mia thought to herself. *This is pitiful. I'm in my early thirties and forgetting things already?*

Everything came back to her remembrance.

Last week during one of their marathon phone conversations, Daryl decided it was time he showed how much he cared about her. He had become weary of talking on the phone all of the time, and chose tonight to take her out.

With all of the changes going on at work and Paula's sudden disappearing act, her date with Daryl Walker totally slipped her mind.

"I'm so sorry, Daryl. Work has been chaotic. I forgot about our date tonight. You caught me just before I was about to take something out of the fridge to cook," Mia said as she escorted him into her spacious living room.

"Forget about cooking, Mia. I'll wait here while you get yourself ready. I made reservations at a restaurant; you're going to love it," Daryl said, while admiring the décor.

"All right, Daryl. I promise I won't take too long. Make yourself comfortable," Mia said as she handed him the remote to her television and headed to her bedroom.

Before getting undressed, Mia tried her sister's phone again. Her call went straight to voice mail.

I can't worry about her tonight, Mia said to herself as she undressed and prepared to hop into the shower.

There's a fine, saved man sitting on my living room sofa waiting for me. Tonight, my focus is going to be on me, and who the Lord may have sent me, Mia said with a smile.

When Mia reentered the living room approximately thirty-five minutes later, Daryl was stunned by the transformation.

In place of the pants, shirt, and jacket she wore to work, Mia changed into a floral dress that showed off her ample physique. She wore strappy black sandals on her feet.

As usual, Mia's naturally curly hair was everywhere.

Daryl rose from the sofa and walked over to where Mia was standing. Grabbing her hand, Daryl looked into Mia's eyes.

"You are a beautiful woman, Mia Wells, and I'm grateful to God for the chance to get to know you," Daryl said.

Mia's thoughts immediately drifted to the day of Jayson and Syrene's wedding—the day she was convinced she would never meet anyone as nice or as caring as Jayson.

Apparently, she was wrong.

Daryl Walker was standing before her; his strong hand holding hers.

"You need to thank God and your sister," Mia said. *"It was Darlene who finally convinced me to give you a chance. She thinks very highly of you. I must admit, thus far, she's been accurate,"* Mia said.

"Mia, you haven't seen anything yet. I'm just getting warmed up!" Daryl answered confidently, revealing a glimpse of his gorgeous smile.

This is going to be a night to remember, Mia said to herself, as Daryl took her hand, and walked her through the front door, commencing their first date.

16

He chose a Mexican restaurant in the Peninsula Town Center in Hampton.

Wow, he didn't impress me as the type of man who would like Mexican food, she said to herself, as he pulled out her chair and helped her get comfortable.

A gentleman, too, she noted as she took in the décor of the dimly lit dining room.

As he settled himself in the seat across from her, she took the time to assess his attire for their first date:

He wore a light gray sweater over charcoal gray pants. He smelled of cologne, a woodsy type of aroma she could not identify. His long eyelashes stood guard over his brown eyes.

Overall, his appearance changed since their first meeting at the church.

Paula initiated the conversation.

"When I first met you, you wanted my sister's number because you wanted to play drums at the church but you never showed up again. What happened?"

Jackson thought for a moment.

What happened was right after I left church my stupid cousin Smokey slipped me a bag of weed and I got arrested and ended up going back to jail for five months. That's what really happened. But I can't tell you that, because if I do, this date will be over immediately, Jackson thought to himself.

He looked at Paula and answered, *"It was my intention to play at the church, but I ended up getting a part-time job at a restaurant that had me working on Sunday mornings. That's why I hadn't been in church. I spoke to your sister about my job situation. She understood, and told me to let her know when my schedule changed.”*

“Speaking of your sister, does she know we are seeing each other?” Jackson asked.

Before Paula could answer, the waiter appeared. Unfamiliar with authentic Mexican cuisine, Paula allowed Jackson to order for the two of them. As soon as the waiter disappeared, Paula answered his question.

“No, I haven't said anything to Mia. Since our mother passed away when we were teenagers, as my older sister, she always felt the need to oversee my personal affairs and relationships. But I'm thirty-one years old now and I'm old enough to handle my own relationships without her intervention and input. Therefore, I'll tell her I'm seeing you when I get ready.”

Jackson nodded in agreement, not only because he felt she was right, but he knew as long as Paula kept quiet about their relationship, their relationship stood a chance.

The remainder of their evening together was very pleasant. The food was delicious, and their conversation flowed easily. Paula found herself talking to Jackson about things she never shared with anyone, particularly her dream of going overseas on a mission trip to care for sick children.

Jackson admired her aspirations, but knew he could not entertain the thought of an overseas mission excursion any time soon. He was on probation and would not be permitted to leave the country.

Paula noticed his sudden change in mood.

"Jackson, what's wrong? Was it something I said?" she asked.

"No, Paula", Jackson answered, perking up. *"My mind drifted. As I listened to your dreams, I remembered the time when I had a few of my own. Seems like so long ago."*

"*Well, go back and get them,*" Paula said as she smiled, reached across the table, and softly touched Jackson's hand. "*It's our dreams that keep us moving forward.*"

Jackson looked down at Paula's hand on top of his and then across the table into her optimistic face.

I could really fall for this woman, Jackson thought to himself.

But then reality awakened him from his momentary state of delusion.

Who am I kidding? Paula and I have so little in common. She has a Master's Degree in Nursing. I may be going to college, but I have an extensive criminal history and am on probation. Heck, when her sister Mia finds out about us, she's going to tell Paula about my background, and I know she'll kick me to the curb, Jackson thought sadly.

I may as well end this tonight.

Jackson suddenly felt stinging pain, as if a hand slapped him in the back of his neck.

He looked behind him.

It had been a hand.

The hand belonged to Matthew Perry, one of his fellow inmates and cooks at the City Jail.

"Well, if it isn't my man, Jackson Braynor!" Matthew roared, attracting the attention of several diners seated nearby in the restaurant.

Jackson stood and embraced his old friend.

"Matt, it's good seeing you! You look great," Jackson said.

A big bear of a man, Matthew Perry had been arrested on an assault charge after causing a near riot in a sports bar during a playoff game.

Matt—a native New Yorker—was a diehard *Giants* fan living in *Redskins* territory. After the police and the ambulance arrived at the bar, Matt was escorted out in handcuffs, headed to the police station, while three of his opponents were wheeled out on gurneys, headed to the emergency room at the hospital.

"Thanks, Jack," Matthew said. *"You're looking pretty good yourself. Let me introduce you to my wife, Cynthia. Cynthia, this is Jack. We met at the city ..."*

Jackson abruptly cut Matthew off. Instead, Jackson shook Cynthia's hand and said, *"It's a pleasure meeting you, Cynthia. Allow me to introduce you to my date, Paula."*

As Cynthia and Paula exchanged polite greetings, Jackson gave Matthew *"the look."* Matthew immediately understood. They both walked off toward the bar.

"She doesn't know, does she?" Matthew said.

"Has no clue," Jackson replied.

"When are you going to tell her, man? She needs to hear it from you," Matthew said.

"I know, Matt, but I'm scared. She's a good woman. I met her in church. She's educated, kind, and sweet. She doesn't run the streets, get high or anything. When she finds out about my past, I know she's not going to want anything to do with me," Jackson said sorrowfully, looking in Paula's direction as she and Matthew's wife chatted comfortably like old friends.

"You don't know that, Jackson. Cynthia is a good woman and she gave me a chance. I wasn't even going to church, but she was," Matthew said.

"Cynthia knew about my past because I'm friends with her brother Jamal. One day, I stopped over his house to see him, and she and I started talking about life. We just hit it off. Of course, Jamal didn't like it at first, but he got over it when he realized I was serious about her. I started going to church with her, gave my life to the Lord, and we got married two years ago. We have a beautiful little boy," Matthew said.

Jackson looked at Paula, who glanced over at him and smiled.

She's beautiful, Jackson thought. *I can't afford to lose her.*

"Jackson, most Christian women are different. They can handle the truth. Tell her about your past, before she finds out from someone else," Matthew urged.

Jackson and Matthew rejoined Paula and Cynthia at the table.

"Guess what, Jackson?" Paula said excitedly. *"Cynthia and I are sorority sisters! We're all going to have to get together again real soon. I'm sure you guys won't mind catching up, either. Where do you know each other from?"*

Jackson's quick-thinking street smarts kicked in.

"We worked in a cafeteria that was operated by the city," Jackson replied, not lying but not telling the whole truth, either.

Matthew glanced at Cynthia, who immediately understood the non-verbal message. She picked up her purse and stood up.

"Paula, it was so nice meeting you, but we have to get going. I'm sure our table is ready, and plus, our babysitter is on the clock," Cynthia said with a smile.

"I do understand, Cynthia. I have your number, and I promise to keep in contact. We'll plan a night out real soon. Nice meeting you, Matthew," Paula said as she waved goodbye.

Jackson returned to his seat at their table, and reached for his glass of water. His mouth suddenly felt parched.

"I didn't know you worked for the city, Jackson," Paula said. *"There's something new I learn about you every day."*

Jackson deposited the glass on the table and looked into Paula's eyes.

"Yes, Paula, there's a lot about me I have yet to share. I just pray that when I do, you'll still be with me, smiling like you are right now," Jackson said.

"Why wouldn't I, Jackson? None of us are perfect. Of course, when we first meet someone, we put our best foot forward. We share all of our best stories. But all of us have a past—a dark side. The Bible says that all have sinned and fall short of the glory of God," Paula said.

"I'm no angel, Jackson. Some of the problems I've had with men were due to the bad choices I made. I knew what I was getting into when I entered into certain relationships, but proceeded anyway, hoping things would work out. I learned the hard way that some people will never change, but I have faith enough to know that truly saved people do," Paula added.

For a fleeting moment, Jackson was tempted to divulge the details of his past to Paula. It seemed as if she opened the door and it was the perfect time to walk through.

However, fear of losing what he stood to gain kept him from doing so.

Jackson remained silent.

The waiter returned to their table.

"Will that be all sir? Coffee, dessert?" he asked.

Jackson looked over at Paula, who shook her head.

"No, thank you. The check please," Jackson said.

As the waiter began to clear the table, Jackson reached over and grabbed Paula's hand. She looked down and smiled.

"Paula, I really enjoyed myself this evening. You are a wonderful woman, and I'm grateful to God for bringing you into my life. I pray I can be the blessing to you that you have already been to me."

Paula tried but could not contain her tears. Slowly, they trickled from her eyes and down her cheeks. Slightly embarrassed, she reached for a napkin. It was too late.

Jackson was wiping them away.

"It's okay, Paula. I understand," Jackson said softly. *"Sometimes I cry, too. After all I've been through, there are times like these—good times—when I become overwhelmed. I've experienced so much pain for so long. But finally, I'm sitting here with someone who's not bringing any pain or any drama into my life."*

"I'm so grateful that God cared enough about me to bring someone like you into my life. Someone who cares about me as a person. Someone who appreciates me for who I am. I understand the tears, Paula. Let them fall," Jackson said.

She looked at him and smiled.

Old things are passed.

17

Jackson walked into the kitchen the following morning and found Reverend Holloway pouring coffee.

"Good morning, Brother Jackson. How are you? How did your date go last night with Sister Paula?" he asked.

As Jackson poured himself a cup of coffee and spooned sugar and coffee creamer into his oversized mug, he related the events of the previous evening, especially his surprise encounter with Matthew Perry.

Reverend Holloway reached into the fridge and pulled out eggs, bacon, and a stick of butter.

"That was a close call, Jackson. When are you planning to tell Paula about your past?" Reverend Holloway asked as he heated a skillet on the stovetop.

Jackson reached into the cabinet and removed two plates and juice glasses.

"I'm afraid, Rev. Paula is a good woman. She's not going to want anything to do with me after she finds out what I've done. I figure if I let her fall in love with me first, it'll be harder for her to walk away when she does find out," Jackson said as he put the plates on the table and reached into a drawer for knives and forks.

"You don't know that, Jackson. You're assuming that everyone you meet has led angelic lives in the past. Look at me. My history is almost as messed up as yours; yet, I got my life together and have been accepted by the woman in my life. Everyone has skeletons in their closets," Reverend Holloway said.

"Secondly, Jackson, you shouldn't begin a relationship based on deception. You're being dishonest with her. You're presenting yourself as a person without serious issues, and that's not the case. Some of your issues are still current, too. You are still on probation. As a saved

man, your relationship must be built on integrity and honesty," Reverend Holloway said.

"You're right, Rev, but Paula has had her share of bad relationships. She's dealt with men with issues and drama. I don't want her to see me as another man with problems," Jackson said.

"She's not going to see you like that, Jackson," Reverend Holloway said, as he began to scramble the eggs.

"Remember what the Bible says, 'If any man be in Christ, he is a new creation. Old things are passed away. Behold! All things are become new'. You're a new man," Reverend Holloway said. "Paula is saved. She's not like the women in the world. The Holy Spirit is going to allow her to 'behold' the new man."

"Let's pray, get ready to eat, and then get to church," Reverend Holloway said. "I don't know about you, but I need a word this morning."

They later drove in silence to the church and pulled into the gravel parking lot. As Sunday School was in session, the lot was half-full.

Jackson opened the car door and stood outside, breathing in the cool fall air. A slight drizzle fell from the overcast sky.

"I'm headed inside," Reverend Holloway announced as he scurried to the door, apparently trying to dodge several drops before they fell upon his natural curly hair.

"You coming?" Reverend Holloway turned and asked.

"Yes, Rev. I'll be right in," Jackson said.

Jackson spotted Paula's car parked near the church's front door. He was having problems focusing on anything. All he could think about was the wonderful time they spent together the evening before.

After they left the restaurant, they drove to Paula's townhouse. For the first time, she invited him inside.

He did not stay long, knowing both of them needed to rise early in the morning for church service.

Paula walked him to the front door and stood before him. He gazed down at the tiny freckles on her face. Her reddish brown hair fell loosely on her shoulders.

He bent down and kissed her lightly on her lips.

"You are a beautiful woman, Paula. I had a wonderful time, and I pray it will not be the last time we spend an evening together," Jackson said.

"I had a good time, too," Paula said. *"It's been years since I have been out on a real date. After being treated so well by you tonight, I'm hopeful again. Thank you, Jackson."*

He smiled, leaned down, and kissed her a second time.

"Goodnight, Paula. I'll see you in church tomorrow morning," Jackson said.

Jackson's mind returned to the present when he heard his name called.

He turned around in time to see Mia approaching him.

"Good morning, Brother Jackson. Glad to see you're able to join us this morning. How have you been?" she asked as she embraced him warmly.

Fighting a spirit of hypocrisy, Jackson returned the embrace.

"I've been doing fine, Sister Mia. I spoke to my boss about working every Sunday so he finally gave me the day off. I'm glad to be back in church today," Jackson said.

"Well, I'm sure glad you're here. I could use you on the drums today. Our regular drummer has a football game this morning. You're right on time, once again. The ram in the bush," Mia announced, patting him on the back.

She looked at her watch. *"Come on, let's go inside, and get set up for service."*

Jackson followed Mia into the sanctuary, walking quietly up the side aisle so not to disturb Deacon Wright as she taught the Adult Sunday School class.

It's gonna take me a minute to get used to women deacons, Jackson said to himself. *I thought I would never see the day.*

As Jackson sat on the stool, arranging the drum set to his satisfaction, he casually looked among the students attending Deacon Wright's class and saw her.

She was sitting on the fourth row. She was easy to spot. Like her sister, Mia, her hair gave her away. It was an unusual color that attracted attention; a mixture of red and brown that changed depending on the sun's exposure. Jackson had never seen anything like it.

Paula caught him staring and smiled. He smiled back and quickly resumed the business at hand. The last thing he needed was Mia taking note of his interaction with her sister. The longer they kept their relationship a secret, the better it would be for the both of them.

The church service was awesome. He had to give it to her; Mia was one of the best musicians and choir directors Jackson ever worked with.

Right before Elder Rhodes preached, the choir sang a song Mia wrote entitled, *"He Did It All."* Not only did her skills as a choir director and a composer surprise him, but so did her choice of a lead singer.

Darlene Walker—dressed as if she was performing at a televised awards show—strode to the front of the choir stand and reached for the cordless microphone.

Her hair was pinned on top of her head, with tendrils cascading down the right side. She wore a purple dress that seemed to be glued to her curvaceous body. Her three-inch heels were of the same hue, as were her manicured nails.

When Darlene opened her mouth to sing, the entire congregation went into shock.

She was not just a pretty face. Darlene Walker could sing!

Almost everyone jumped to his or her feet, which encouraged Darlene to take her singing to the next level.

She took several steps forward, put her left hand on her hip as she held the microphone with her right hand and sang:

"When I was hungry God fed, me; Lost, God, led me. I was blind, God made me see; Down, God lifted me..."

It was over! Darlene Walker and the Wayside Church Choir were witnessing through their musical selection what everyone in the church must have experienced.

God did it all!

In essence, it was a musical praise report, and when the song was over, it was time for a praise break!

Darlene Walker—in her three-inch heels—took off running with the cordless microphone down the center aisle as if she was running the last leg of the four by one hundred meter relay race. Several members in the congregation ran behind her, while some of the choir members began dancing for joy.

The ushers had their hands full, especially the males; making sure several of the heavyset people in the congregation did not destroy the seats in the sanctuary while giving God praise.

Mother Williams slowly rose from her seat with her cane. As quickly as she could, she tossed a sheet over a young woman who fell out near the front of the church, covering her legs from the gawking eyes of several of the young men seated nearby.

Deacon Sam sprang into action as well after Elder Rhodes decided not to preach, and instead called for prayer.

Deacon Sam stood at his side as he anointed with oil those who came to the altar, laid hands on them, and prayed.

As the power of the Holy Spirit flowed through the sanctuary, Jackson suddenly stopped playing, and buried his head in his hands. He was overwhelmed.

Growing up as a minister's son, Jackson was aware of the great change God could make in a person's life. He witnessed what God did in the life of his own father, who had been an alcoholic for years, and his mother, who prayed until the Lord delivered him.

Amid the praise, Jackson heard the Voice of the Lord.

"There are women who love like your mother does. You found one. Trust Me, Jackson. Paula will not turn her back on you. Old things are passed away."

From the band section, Jackson looked among the crowd of worshippers still in high praise.

He saw Paula. She was looking directly at him. Tears were streaming down her face.

He wanted so badly to go to her, but he knew better. It wasn't the time to expose their relationship. Paula and Mia may have had the same parents, but they didn't seem to have the same heart.

While Paula was kind, warm, and free-spirited, Mia's occupation left her hard and skeptical.

Jackson believed Mia would undoubtedly do all she could to keep him away from her beloved sister.

As things began to settle down in the sanctuary, Elder Rhodes extended the invitation to Christian Discipleship and church membership.

Jackson stood and made his way to the front of the church. He had joined the music ministry at Wayside, but had not officially become a member..

Elder Rhodes grabbed Jackson's hand and embraced him, as did Reverend Holloway, who—along with the rest of the ministers—stood with him at the altar.

It seemed as if Jackson's walk to the altar triggered a movement.

One by one, others began to join him at the altar, many crying, accompanied by friends or relatives. It was an awesome harvest of souls that morning.

At the conclusion of the service, as Jackson returned to the band section to cover the drum set and assist Mia in securing the rest of the musical equipment, he felt a tap on his shoulder.

Turning around, he found himself face to face with Daryl Walker.

"Welcome to Wayside, my brother!" Daryl said with a smile as he embraced Jackson. *"I was wondering when you were going to join us. You made the right move, my man!"*

"Thanks, Brother Daryl. I agree," Jackson said, looking over Daryl's shoulder in search of Paula. *"Ever since I came here, I felt comfortable, like I belong here. After today's service, I knew it."*

"Yeah, it was bedlam up in here today. I haven't seen church this lit in years. The Holy Spirit really moved in the house this morning. Anyway, I'm not going to keep you because I see you have a lot to do. But as leader of the Men's Fellowship, I just wanted to officially welcome you to Wayside. Next Saturday we are having our annual Men's Fellowship Breakfast. I hope you'll be able to join us," Daryl said, handing him a flyer for the breakfast and a business card with his cell phone number on it.

After a few minutes of small talk, Jackson thanked him, and Daryl walked away.

It feels good to be finally meeting other men who aren't about the street life, Jackson said to himself as he pocketed Daryl's information.

Old things are passing away.

18

Keeping with her Sunday tradition, Mia arrived at Paula's townhouse after church for dinner.

She hung her jacket in the hall closet, walked to the kitchen, reached into the refrigerator for a can of soda, plopped herself in front of the television in the living room, and flipped through the channels for a football game.

"Church was amazing today, wasn't it?" Mia said as she sipped her soda and settled on a game between the *Giants* and the *Cowboys.*

"It really was. Darlene Walker shocked everybody. I had no idea she could sing like that," Paula said, reaching underneath the cabinet for her electric mixer.

"I'm not going to lie, I didn't either. Her brother was the one who told me to give her a solo. I thought Darlene was just in the choir for attention. I had no idea she had a voice. He told me she could sing, so I taught her a song I wrote. She came to rehearsal and laid it out. We knew what was going to happen when you all heard her this morning," Mia said.

"You wrote that song, Mia? You have skills, Sis! You certainly picked the perfect song for her. Seems like she was getting into it, as if the song was her own personal testimony," Paula said.

"It kind of was, Paula. Without putting Darlene's personal business out there, she's been through a lot. Her beauty has attracted a lot of negative attention from men, so much so that Daryl told me he has to step away or he will end up hurting someone. After all, she is his twin, and his only sibling, so only God knows the connection they developed in the womb," Mia said.

"That's the truth, Mia. We're not even twins but share a deep connection as siblings," Paula said as she donned two potholders and reached into the oven to remove a pan of baked chicken.

"So, Paula, where were you last night?" Mia asked coolly, her eyes still focused on the football game. "I must have called your phone about seven times and I kept getting your voice mail."

Paula paused. She knew this moment was coming.

She was prepared.

"I met up with one of my sorority sisters named Cynthia. Our sorority has a code of conduct that stipulates whenever we are together, we turn off our phones," Paula said.

She didn't exactly lie.

"Oh, that must have been nice. Where did you go?" Mia asked.

"We went to a Mexican restaurant in the Peninsula Town Center. The food was pretty good," Paula said, still telling the truth.

"I didn't know you like Mexican food, Paula. We're going to have to check it out one day," Mia said.

I can't wait, Paula said to herself.

"Well, let me tell you about my night, Paula," Mia said, as she rose from the sofa, went into the kitchen, grabbed a plate and began to spoon mashed potatoes and green beans onto it. Afterward, Paula forked two plump chicken legs onto Mia's plate.

Mia described her date with Daryl in detail. First, he took her to a seafood restaurant in downtown Hampton, and later they stopped at a jazz club. She obviously had a great time, because her face was aglow as she jabbered on and on about him.

Paula was genuinely happy for her sister, especially after her breakup with Jayson. Daryl seemed like the perfect person to bring Mia out of her dating slump; he was saved, energetic, outgoing, and handsome.

"Mia, I'm so happy for you, and I'm glad to see you smiling again. It seems like Daryl is a good match for you," Paula said. *"What do you think?"*

Hesitating for a moment, Mia said, *"You know, I think we have potential, Paula. He's so easygoing and open about everything. I don't think there's anything we couldn't honestly discuss. The most important thing is already covered. Daryl loves the Lord. Nothing else really matters, does it?"*

"No," Paula said. *"No one is perfect, Mia. We have to accept the fact that all of us have issues. And once we get saved, old things are passed away."*

"You're right, Sis. Whatever is in our past needs to stay there! It's time to focus on the future," Mia announced.

19

The Men's Ministry held their annual buffet breakfast the following Saturday morning. Fortunately, Jackson didn't have to work, so he was able to attend.

There were about forty-five men in attendance of various ages, many of whom were guests from other churches.

Upon their arrival, the attendees were handed a black felt-tipped pen, which they used to write their names on a nametag. Afterward, they were directed to the buffet where they waited in line to be served.

This reminds me of jail, Jackson chuckled to himself.

He heard a voice behind him.

"Hey, Brother Jackson. Glad you could make it!"

It was Daryl Walker.

"Hey Brother Daryl. That makes two of us. I'm glad I didn't have to work this morning. Unfortunately, I'll have to work tomorrow so I'll miss service, but I'm here now," Jackson said with a grin.

"That's all that matters, Jackson. Get your food, and come sit next to me. We have a good speaker this morning. You're going to enjoy him," Daryl said as he walked off to greet other guests.

Jackson's stomach began to growl as he inspected the food laid out before him. There were scrambled eggs, grits, toast, pancakes, waffles, ham, bacon, sausages, potatoes, biscuits, muffins, and assorted fresh fruits.

Someone in a chef's hat was preparing an omelet. Juices, coffee, and tea were available on another table.

Wayside certainly knows how to prepare a breakfast buffet, Jackson noted. *I'm impressed.*

After everyone had eaten, Daryl approached the podium and introduced the preacher, his former pastor from New York. The men's chorus sang a selection, and Elder Nicholas Soto, Pastor of the Agape Christian Church of the Bronx, stood before the assembly of men.

After a customary greeting and prayer, Elder Soto read the scripture, 2nd Corinthians 5:17, and announced his subject: *"It's All About Newness!"*

"Right here in this fellowship hall, there are men who have been delivered from things that took place in their past. Some have been delivered from violent acts. Some have been delivered from drug abuse and others from alcoholism.

Some of you have been delivered from criminality and suicidal thoughts.

Yet, with all of this deliverance, there are still those of you who come to church Sunday after Sunday, bound by the guilt of past sins and dealing with fallout from past behaviors.

However, the Lord sent me here to tell you that when your past decides to show up in your present, you can say, 'I don't know anything about that—old things have passed away! It's all about newness!'

My brothers, when we gave our lives over to the Lord, there were several things that we received in the process. On this morning, I am going to start with my favorite passage of scripture and preach on one of the things we received when we got saved: Newness!

In our text for this morning, the apostle Paul is going to help us separate ourselves from our past. He wrote these words to the new believers in the church at Corinth, recorded in 2nd Corinthians 5:17, 'Therefore, if anyone is in Christ, he is a new creation; old things have passed away; behold, all things have become new.'

First of all, please note that the apostle declared, 'Anyone'. Anyone means just that; anyone. The invitation is inclusive. It is not based on your lineage or parentage. It is not based on your income or heritage. Anyone means anyone!

As we continue, the Apostle declared, 'if anyone is in Christ, he is a new creation'. Therefore, after you gave your life to the Lord, you became a new creation.

No matter how old you were when you came to the Lord, your life restarted at that moment. It was a rebirth. It was a new beginning.

This is the essence of what the Bible teaches about regeneration. From a biological standpoint, regeneration is defined as 'the restoration or the new growth of a living organism that had been lost, removed or injured'.

Let me see if I can make this live... everyone in here has skin, hair, and nails. Your skin, hair and nails are living organisms. When you cut yourself, did you notice that the skin over the cut grows back after a while? When you cut your hair or your nails, they grow back. You don't have to go and buy a hair or nail replacement kit and glue nails on your fingers or weave hair into your scalp. It grows back on its own. That is the process of regeneration. It grows back, and that which grows back is new. It's new skin...new nails...new hair...

If our wives were here, they would know what I am talking about. When they get a perm, after a while they have to go back and get what is called a 'touch up', because new hair eventually begins to grow back.

When the new hair (the regenerated hair) begins to grow, it is not as straight as the permed hair, because the permed hair was treated by chemicals. When the regenerated hair—the new hair—grows in, you can tell the difference (so can we!!!). That is why we have to give them money to go back to the salon and get a touch-up. The purpose for the touchup is to make the regenerated hair look just like the permed hair.

Well, Paul said, 'if anyone be in Christ, he is a new creation...' As this applies to you and I, once we gave our lives to the Lord, He began to cut away and remove that which was old and diseased. He began to cut away our old way of thinking. He began to cut away our old way of living. Our old behaviors and old attitudes and old actions were cut away, and the process of regeneration began.

198

That's why the old saints used to say, 'I looked at my hands, and my hands looked new...I looked at my feet and they did, too!' Whoever that person was before your regeneration, that is not who you are anymore. You are new!

Now, although the Word clearly states in 2 Corinthians 5:17, 'Old things are passed away; behold, all things are become new,' a problem exists for most of us.

Like we said before, you have undergone the process of regeneration spiritually; the old you and all that it represented has been surgically removed by the Holy Spirit the moment you gave your life to the Lord. Immediately, the Holy Spirit removed your sins and then began the process of cutting away old, diseased behaviors and attitudes.

But while the Lord is performing this spiritual surgical procedure, the enemy is hovering around, retrieving that which has been cut away and is attempting to reattach it to you!

All of you have heard of situations when a person was involved in an accident, and one of their limbs—their fingers or arms or legs were cut off in the accident. The emergency medical service team members take the severed arm or finger, wrap it in ice, and bring it along with the patient to the hospital, where surgeons will attempt to reattach it to the body. They have to do that, because the arms, fingers, toes, and legs will not regenerate themselves. A person cannot grow a new arm; therefore, the old one must be reattached.

I brought this up, because the enemy has convinced some of you that there is no spiritual process of regeneration. The enemy is trying to convince you that you are going to need all of that stuff that the Lord cut away.

Therefore, the enemy picked up that which the Lord cut off, 'packed it in ice,' and has been trying to reattach it to you ever since! The enemy told you that you have to take your old ways back, because you cannot grow or develop any new ones.

The enemy has convinced you that your attitude will never change, because that is just the way you are! It's part of your nature; it's part of your personality! It's who you are, and you can't develop a new attitude or a new nature or a new personality! He has convinced you that you may as well let him reattach that old attitude and that old nature and those old behaviors, because you will not develop any new ones!

I am talking to someone this morning. When you gave your life to the Lord, the Lord cut away your old addictions and habits, but the enemy has been running behind you, trying to reattach those habits. He is trying to convince you that you cannot make it without smoking weed, you cannot function without a drink or a drug!

When you gave your life to the Lord, He cut away your old promiscuous behavior, but the enemy has been chasing you down, trying to reattach that behavior. He is trying to convince you that are not a one-woman man. You have always been a player, and you will always be one.

When you gave your life to the Lord, the Lord cut away your old negative attitudes and behaviors, but the enemy has been chasing you down, trying to reattach those behaviors. The enemy is trying to convince you that you need to cuss folks out and slap folks around in order to get respect.

But the devil is a liar! The Lord cut that stuff away from you for a reason, The Lord cut it—He removed it—because He is making room for new growth!

And you need to know this morning that whatever the Lord starts, He is going to finish, for the word declares in Philippians 1:6, 'Being confident of this very thing, that he who has begun a good work in you will complete it until the day of Jesus Christ.'

Therefore, you need to stand in confidence and know that there is something new growing inside of you every day.

The Lord is doing a new thing in your life! A new attitude is developing. A new walk is developing!

From this day forward, do not worry about what happened in the past.

My brother, you are in Christ!.
You are a new creation!
Don't let anybody drag up your past!
Old things are passed away!
Behold. All things are become new!
It is all about newness today!
Somebody give God praise up in here!"

Most of the men in the room stood on their feet and began to clap their hands. Several were wiping tears from their eyes, obviously moved by the message.

Elder Soto headed toward his seat, but suddenly turned around. He looked over the crowd of men, some in tears and others with their heads buried in their folded arms on the table.

"I hear the Lord speaking to me," Elder Soto proclaimed. *"There are several men in the room who are shackled by their past. It's time to let it go. If I am talking to you, I need you to come down front."*

There was a small stampede to the makeshift altar. Just about every man had left his seat and was standing before Elder Soto.

Men in suits and ties. Men in jeans and sneakers. Even Elder Rhodes was standing there, with his hands lifted and eyes closed.

They huddled together, holding hands in front of the altar, like football players awaiting the next play from their quarterback.

Jackson glanced to his left; Daryl was standing there, holding his hand but barely holding his emotions together.

"Whatever it is, Brother Daryl, let it go. You heard the preacher. Old things have passed away," Jackson whispered.

Daryl looked at Jackson and suddenly released himself from Jackson's grasp. He turned and walked away.

Out of the corner of his eye, Jackson watched as Daryl walked past the restroom to the door leading to the parking lot. Without looking back, Daryl walked out. The door closed behind him.

Jackson released the hand of the man standing to his right and followed Daryl. He caught up with him as he was about to get into his car.

"*Where are you going, Daryl?*" Jackson asked quietly.

"*I can't do this anymore, Jackson. I can't. I heard what the preacher said, but I can't let it go,*" Daryl said, as the tears continued to spill from his swollen eyes.

Jackson thought for a moment. No one at Wayside knew of his past except Pastor Holloway and Mia. It was his preference to keep it that way; however, God had another plan.

"*Daryl, I don't know what's going on with you, but let me tell you something. When I first came to this church, I got off the bus straight from the County Jail,*" Jackson said. "*I'm surprised most of you don't remember me. It was me who played the drums for your choir when you sang at the jail.*"

Daryl looked up and into the eyes of Jackson, who was standing near his car door.

"*I never made the connection, Jackson. I don't recognize you from the service at the jail. Maybe because you were in your prison jumpsuit when I first saw you, I don't know,"* Daryl said sadly. *"What I do know is that your past has nothing to do with mine. I did a horrible thing, Jackson."*

Daryl turned away and looked into the distance.

Jackson's response interrupted the silence.

"Come on, bro. It can't be that bad," he said.

When Daryl returned from his trance, he said two words:

"Get in."

They drove off the church grounds and Daryl began sharing the events of his past with Jackson Braynor.

20

Jackson sat on the sofa in his basement apartment later that afternoon. His mind was on Daryl Walker's shocking revelation.

He would have never known that Daryl had it in him.

Reverend Holloway was right, Jackson recalled. *We all have issues.*

Moreover, Jackson was surprised that Daryl chose to disclose the details to him. It wasn't as if they were close friends or even acquaintances. They just met the previous Sunday after Jackson joined Wayside.

Jackson rose from the sofa and walked across his small, windowless living room.

Why me? Was it because I happened to be there? Perhaps it was after I told him I had been to jail that let him know I have issues, too, Jackson pondered, trying to make sense of the timing of Daryl's confession.

Whatever the reason, it was now out in the open.

Jackson knew Daryl Walker's past, and it did not change his feelings toward Daryl. If anything, he admired him the more.

Like himself, and Reverend Holloway, Daryl was an overcomer. He apparently refused to allow his past to define his present.

Daryl persevered and became a man anyone would be proud to call a friend.

I'm honored to know him. If Daryl overcame, so can I, Jackson asserted.

Across town, however, it was a different story.

Daryl Walker was still sitting in his car, which was parked in front of his apartment building. The events of the morning had totally caught him unaware.

He left his apartment that morning, headed to the church for the Men's fellowship breakfast. As the ministry leader, all he planned to do was make sure everything ran smoothly from beginning to end.

Of course, he was looking forward to seeing Elder Soto and spending time with him before he headed back to New York later that afternoon.

Instead, the Spirit of the Lord made an appearance at the breakfast, and Daryl's plans shifted.

He had no idea what happened near the end of the message. By the time Elder Soto summoned the men to the altar, Daryl could no longer contain his emotions.

Every time he heard the word *"past"*, it brought things to the present Daryl wanted to keep buried forever.

Elder Soto's powerful message and altar call dragged Daryl's *"baggage"* out of the closet where he had stuffed it years ago. With nowhere to hide it, Daryl found himself doing something he promised he would never do.

He opened it in front of someone else.

No one, except his sister, Darlene, and his mother knew what happened over ten years prior. Shortly after the matter had been resolved in court, Daryl and Darlene—both eighteen at the time—were accepted into a college in Virginia.

While their mother remained in New York, they remained in Virginia until they received their degrees in Physical Therapy, and eventually settled in Hampton.

Initially, they secured jobs in different hospitals, but in time they decided to open their own practice, which had become quite prosperous.

Hence, no one in the State of Virginia knew of Daryl Walker's past.

Until now.

Jackson Braynor knows, Daryl said to himself, his hands gripping the steering wheel. *Who could he tell? He's a criminal himself. It's not as if we know the same people and hang out in the same circles. What do I have to worry about?*

Daryl finally got out of his car and headed to his apartment.

He was not the least bit surprised to hear footsteps running toward the front door as soon as he unlocked it. His dog, Buster, had been watching him from the window ever since his car pulled into his assigned parking space. Daryl knew what to expect as soon as he walked in.

Buster galloped toward Daryl, who grabbed his leash, hooked it to the dog's collar, turned, and headed back outdoors.

Buster's pedigree was open for discussion. He was a mutt for sure, part golden retriever, hound, Labrador retriever, German Shepherd and goodness knows what else. Daryl found him at the local shelter and gave him a forever home.

"Okay, Buster, we're not walking all over town today. Just handle your business and we're heading back indoors," Daryl said, sorry he did not grab a warmer jacket on his way out.

As Daryl walked behind Buster, he couldn't shake the feeling of dread. Although he felt somewhat liberated by sharing his past with Jackson, he was still unsure if he made the right decision.

Maybe I better call him and remind him to keep my secret between us, Daryl thought.

After Buster lifted his hind leg and emptied his bladder against his favorite fire hydrant, Daryl turned and headed back to his apartment.

As soon as he unlocked the front door and unhooked the leash from Buster's collar, Daryl sat down on his sofa.

Buster joined him.

How could I have been so foolish? Daryl said to Buster, who only wagged his tail in response.

He dialed Jackson's number and waited nervously until he answered.

21

"*Sounds as if you all had an awesome fellowship breakfast this morning*", Paula texted from under the dryer at the hair salon.

"*I've been to church breakfasts before, but nothing quite like that,*" Jackson texted back. "*It was like a Sunday morning worship service.*"

Suddenly, Jackson's screen changed. A call was coming in.

It was Daryl Walker.

"*Paula, I'm going to get back to you in a few. I have a call coming in,*" Jackson texted.

"*Sure, where am I going? My hair is still wet,*" Paula texted.

Jackson answered the phone.

"*Hello? Daryl?*" Jackson said.

Relieved, Daryl replied, "*Hey bro. How are you?*"

"*I'm good Bro. How about yourself?*" Jackson asked casually.

"*I'm okay,*" Daryl said. "*Still recovering from the breakfast this morning. I'm not going to keep you. Look, I know I probably don't need to say this, but what I shared with you this morning was something I never told anyone. I'm trusting you to keep it to yourself.*"

"*Daryl, you don't have to worry about that,*" Jackson said. "*I'm not going to say a word to anyone. With my criminal history, I'm in no position to talk about anybody else, but even if I was, I wouldn't do it. I'm not that type of person.*"

I mind my business, Bro. You don't ever have to worry about me. I got your back."

"Alright, then. Well, I guess I'll see you in rehearsal next Thursday. Take care, Bro, and thanks again for being there for me this morning," Daryl said.

"I'm humbled that you feel I'm worthy of your trust. I won't let you down, Daryl. Have a blessed day," Jackson said.

"You too, Bro," Daryl said as he disconnected the call.

Jackson was about to text Paula back when he glanced at the clock on the wall.

Dang. I have to meet Reverend Holloway at the homeless shelter in thirty minutes! I'll text Paula back when I get on the bus, Jackson said to himself.

He hurried to his bedroom, changed clothes, grabbed his keys, rushed out of the door, and ran to the bus stop.

Fortunately, the bus was a few minutes late. Upon its arrival, Jackson boarded, paid the fare, and found a window seat near the front of the bus. He reached into his jacket pocket for his phone.

It wasn't there.

He began to pat himself down.

No phone.

Then he remembered.

I left my phone on the table!

I promised Paula I would text her back. She's probably thinking I'm up to no good by now, Jackson lamented.

Jackson's thoughts picked up speed along with the bus.

Heck, I can't even use Reverend Holloway's phone because I don't know Paula's number by heart. It's stored in my phone, he groaned to himself.

Angry at himself, Jackson turned and stared out of the window. He tried to remain positive, but the "*Doomsday Committee*" that periodically meets inside his head decided to host a call meeting during the short bus ride across town.

"You blew it again, Jackson! Paula is going to think you're a player! By the time you get back to her, it's going to be late this evening. Suddenly getting off the phone was sketchy anyway. You didn't even tell her who was calling. You just stopped texting her all of a sudden and virtually disappeared for the rest of the day. Shaaady!!!" one of the *'Committee Members'* sneered.

"Truthfully, if you ask us, we don't know why you even thought she would take you seriously anyway. Look at you, Jackson! You're a thug. A hoodlum! Straight outta jail! We gotta give it to you, though; you tried to dress yourself up and put on a good show, but after today, you can hang it up! She won't be talking to you after this little stunt. 'I left my phone home.' Yeah, right! the "*Committee Members*'" taunted. *"Oldest excuse in the book!"*

By the time Jackson got off the bus, he had a headache. His already fragile self-worth had taken a beating by *"The Committee."*

Reverend Holloway noticed the cloud hovering over Jackson's head as soon as he entered the building.

"Jackson, what's the matter?" Reverend Holloway asked.

Jackson lied.

"Nothing, Rev. I'm good," Jackson said as he removed his jacket.

"You sure? You look as if you've been handed bad news," Reverend Holloway said.

"No, Rev. I'm good. Where do you need me today?" Jackson asked, manufacturing a smile in an attempt to shake the cloak of depression that attached itself to him.

"You can start in the kitchen. I'm sure they need help in there," Reverend Holloway said.

"Okay, Rev," Jackson said as he headed toward the back.

Reverend Holloway studied Jackson as he donned an apron and walked over to the sink to wash his hands.

Something is bothering him. I'll get him to tell me during the drive home, Reverend Holloway said to himself.

22

Paula was flipping through magazines while waiting for her hair to dry when she looked up and saw a familiar face entering the salon.

Darlene Walker strutted through the front door as if she owned the place.

You have to love her, Paula smiled.

Darlene removed her large dark sunglasses from her perfectly made-up face and deposited them in a black leather case. Surprisingly, after announcing her arrival to the receptionist, Darlene made her way over to where Paula was sitting.

Everything about Darlene was in order, including her hair.

Paula wondered why Darlene scheduled an appointment. Her hair looked beautiful.

"Hi Paula. I didn't know you came here," Darlene said.

"Hi Darlene. Yes, I've been coming to this shop since I moved here from New York. I usually don't come on Saturdays. That's probably why you never saw me," Paula said.

"Well, I'm glad to see a friendly face in here," Darlene said while glaring at several women who were staring at her with hostility.

"As a matter of fact, I understand we're almost family, with your sister and my brother dating each other," Darlene said, beaming.

"So I heard," Paula said.

"I hooked them up, you know," Darlene announced proudly. "I love my brother. He's a really good guy. Your sister is a blessed woman to grab a fine man like him."

"Keeping it real," Darlene continued, "I hand-picked your sister for my brother. After I heard what happened with her last relationship, I was blown away. I don't know many women who would have done what she did. I wanted a woman like that to be with my brother."

"You're right, Darlene," Paula replied. "For a while, I thought Mia had lost her mind. Jayson was a very good man, and for the life of me, I couldn't understand why she just gave him up the way she did. She was better than me."

"Me, too, Paula. As hard as it is to find a good man? Please! There is no way in the world Darlene Walker would give my man up. That would not happen!" Darlene said a little too loudly, as if to make a point to the other women in the salon who continued to stare at her with envy.

"I truly understand, Darlene," Paula agreed quietly.

Shifting her attention back to Paula, Darlene asked, *"So, what about you? Do you need me to hook you up? As you can see, I'm a pretty good matchmaker."*

"No, that's all right, Darlene. I can handle my own love life," Paula said graciously.

"You sure, Paula? You've been at Wayside for a couple of years now. I've never seen you even talking to anybody," Darlene said.

Paula replied jokingly, *"Come to think of it, Darlene, I haven't seen you talking to anybody either. You're all up in my business; what's your story?"*

A slight blush appeared on Darlene's cheeks.

"Let's just say I like to keep my options open," Darlene answered. *"I enjoy dating, but I discovered that once a relationship begins to get serious, in comes the drama. I would prefer to enjoy a man's company without all of the*

problems that come with a relationship, you know what I mean?"

"It's not like that with all relationships Darlene," Paula said. "While that may have been the case with a lot of women we know, I watched Mia and her former fiancé enjoy a wonderful, uncomplicated relationship that even included his son at one point. Drama does not have to be a part of every relationship."

Darlene pondered Paula's statement for a moment.

"I don't know, Paula. Maybe you're right. Perhaps it's the type of men I attract. All they seem to want is ownership of me, as if I'm a possession rather than a person. That's such a turn-off," Darlene said.

Peering under the hood of the dryer, Paula said, "Darlene, did it ever occur to you that maybe you are presenting yourself as a possession rather than a person?"

"What do you mean?" Darlene asked innocently.

Paula turned slightly in her chair to face Darlene before she spoke.

"Look at you. You're the picture of perfection all of the time. While most of us are dressed in casual attire today, you came waltzing in here as if it was Saturday night instead of Saturday morning. Who comes to a hair salon with their hair done already?"

Paula continued. *"Darlene, you are on 'ten' all of the time. When men look at you, they see you as a showpiece. They're not bothering to look any deeper. They treat you as a trophy to possess, because that's the woman you have presented to them. But when you present Darlene 'the real woman,' I guarantee you, things will begin to change in your relationships with men."*

Darlene was very quiet. For a moment, Paula was afraid she hurt her feelings, but Darlene suddenly lifted the dryer's hood, reached down, and hugged Paula.

"Paula, you're right! Thank you so much! No one's ever told me the truth about myself," Darlene said, wiping moisture from her eyes.

"I don't have any real friends, Paula. Real friends tell you what you need to hear, not what you want to hear. I needed to hear what you said today. I hope today will be the beginning of a real friendship," Darlene said.

"I would like that, too, Darlene. I like you. With all the makeup and hair and beautiful clothes and high-heeled shoes, I know there is a real, warm person inside," Paula said.

"Here's my cell number. Call me anytime, and let's get together real soon and do lunch or something, okay?" Paula added.

Darlene beamed as she tapped Paula's number into her phone. She hugged Paula again just as she heard the receptionist announce, "Darlene Walker! We're ready for you!"

"I have to go. Thanks again, Paula, and I will call you. I promise," Darlene said.

"Please do, Darlene. See you in church tomorrow," Paula said.

"Okay, Paula. Be blessed," Darlene said as she smiled and strutted away.

Paula watched as Darlene sat in her stylist's chair and began to engage in conversation with her.

Wow. You really don't know a person until you talk to them, Paula thought to herself.

Paula looked at her phone. While she and Darlene chatted at length, she expected Jackson to have texted her back.

He had not.

No big deal, Paula thought as she continued to flip through her magazines.

Something obviously came up.

He'll get back to me soon. He always does.

By the time Paula left the salon and was in her car, headed home, her thoughts toward Jackson were beginning to take a turn. Almost two hours had passed since she heard from him.

At every red light, she picked up her cell phone.

No incoming calls or text messages from Jackson.

She reread his last message at least six times.

Paula, I'm going to text you back in a few. I have to take this call.

Every block she travelled—every hour that passed without word from him—the cloud thickened over her once carefree thoughts about him.

I knew this was too good to be true, Paula said to herself as she pulled into her assigned parking space in front of her townhouse.

Another liar, Paula said aloud angrily. *I don't have time for this*, as she slammed her car door and walked to her house.

23

"*Okay, what is it, Jackson?*" Reverend Holloway asked as they drove away from the homeless shelter.

Jackson was slumped in the passenger seat, gazing at the drizzle that had accumulated on the passenger side window.

"*It's nothing, Rev, really,*" Jackson answered, trying his best to sound nonchalant.

Reverend Holloway wasn't buying it.

"*Jackson, I know you. You're too quiet. What happened?*" Reverend Holloway persisted.

Jackson exhaled and explained the events of his day.

"Is that all, Jackson? Surely, you don't think Paula is so small-minded that she's not going to understand once you explain to her what happened. She's not like the young girls in the street you're used to dealing with. They are clueless and tend to act before they think. Paula is a woman with class and intelligence. She'll understand as soon as you tell her what happened," Reverend Holloway said.

"Secondly, you need to do something about your 'Committee!' That's ridiculous! Those negative thoughts in your head shouldn't have that much control over you. You are a child of the King! God is doing a new thing in your life; old things are passed away! The 'Committee' needs to catch the vision or go somewhere and sit down!" Reverend Holloway declared in his *"preacher's"* voice.

The dark cloud that had been hovering all afternoon over Jackson's head was finally dispersing. He began to straighten up in his seat.

"You know, Rev, you're right," Jackson admitted. *"It's not that serious. What was I thinking? Paula will*

understand. Just in that moment, doubt began to arise because nothing ever turned out right before in my life."

"I need to understand that this really is a new season," Jackson continued. *"This really is a new chapter in my life. I've given my life to the Lord Jesus. I have to expect things to turn out right,"* Jackson said.

"That's right," Reverend Holloway said. *"You're meeting different people and encountering different experiences. Therefore, you need to expect different outcomes."*

"Thanks, Rev, for always being here to encourage me," Jackson said.

"It's part of my ministry, Jackson. Ministering doesn't only take place Sunday morning from the pulpit. It's an everyday assignment for me," Reverend Holloway replied.

"Uh, Rev, could you speed it up a little? I need to get home so I can call Paula!" Jackson said with a laugh.

"You got it!" Reverend Holloway answered while pressing his foot a little harder on the gas pedal.

The moment Reverend Holloway steered his car into the driveway, Jackson said goodbye, bolted from the car, and ran into his basement apartment to call Paula.

He was out of breath by the time she answered the phone.

"Hello?" Paula said.

Jackson paused momentarily. The reality that faced him almost brought a tear to his eye.

Paula saw my name on her caller ID and answered the phone.

She wants to hear from me!

"Paula, hi. I'm so, so sorry that I'm just getting back to you," Jackson said.

He proceeded to explain what happened, beginning with the phone call from Daryl that interrupted the text messaging between the two of them, and his ultimately running out of the house without his phone.

Jackson was even honest enough to share with Paula the misery he experienced after *"The Committee"* convened.

Paula sat and listened to him. Immediately, a sense of relief swept over her as well. The negative thoughts that infiltrated her mind were almost equivalent to his, although there was no *"committee meeting."*

She too had struggled with doubts. It had been years since she dated. She was finally beginning to let her guard down with Jackson, but his sudden disappearing act had left her feeling as if she might have made a mistake in doing so.

His explanation allowed her to breathe easier.

He is a good man with good intentions, she thought to herself. *I wasn't wrong after all!*

"I appreciate your calling and explaining to me what happened today. It eased much of my concern," Paula said.

"I'm sorry I left you feeling uneasy, Paula. It wasn't my intention," Jackson said apologetically. "Anyway, how did the rest of your day go?"

Without divulging the details of their conversation, Paula told Jackson of her meeting Darlene in the beauty shop earlier that morning.

"That must have been interesting. I've only seen her a couple of times; she seems like a real character," Jackson said.

"I thought so, too, until I had a chance to talk to her," Paula said. "She's really a sweet person; just misunderstood."

"Aren't we all?" Jackson said.

"What do you mean?" Paula asked.

235

"Nothing. I was just thinking out loud. Look, it's getting late and I have to get up in the morning and go to work. I'm sorry I won't make it to church, but I hope to talk to you sometime tomorrow afternoon when I get off," Jackson said.

"I look forward to it, Jackson. Have a good night, and thanks again for calling me," Paula said prior to disconnecting the call.

She placed the phone on her bed and walked into her master bath. Sprinkling bath salts into the tub, she turned on the hot water and walked back into her bedroom to remove her clothes.

As she listened to the water running, she heard the Voice.

Old things are passed away.

What am I doing? she thought to herself. *I'm a grown woman, capable of making my own decisions.*

Paula picked up the phone and made a call. After she hung up, she smiled, removed her clothes, walked into the bathroom, and sank into the warm soapy water in the tub.

24

Paula was inspecting the pot roast in the slow cooker when the doorbell rang.

She looked at her watch.

Mia's here already? They must have had a guest preacher today, Paula said to herself. *Elder Rhodes is longwinded.*

"Coming," Paula yelled, as she headed to the front door.

She peered through the glass on the side of the door and opened it.

"Oh, you're early," Paula said as she smiled.

"I hope you don't mind. I didn't feel like driving across town to change and then back over here."

"*You know I don't mind at all,*" Paula said as she turned to close and lock the front door.

"*It smells wonderful in here. What's that I smell?*"

Before Paula could answer, her front door was pushed in. Mia blew past Paula as a gust of wind, talking a mile a minute.

When Mia strode into the living room, she froze as if someone held a loaded gun to her head.

"*Hello Sister Mia,*" he said.

Mia did not respond. Instead, she turned and looked at her sister, who was locking the front door.

"*Paula, what is he doing here?*" Mia asked.

Instead of answering her question, Paula responded, "*Mia, I believe Jackson spoke to you.*"

Mia looked at Paula as if she had lost her mind.

239

"*And I believe I asked you a question, Paula.   What is he doing here?*" Mia repeated.

Jackson moved toward the door.

"*I'm going to leave, Paula,*" he said.

"*Good idea,*" Mia responded sarcastically, as she walked ahead of him to the front door, opened it, and stepped aside.

"*No, you're not, Jackson,*" Paula said as she grabbed his right arm. "*I invited you here, and you're staying,*" Paula said.

"*You invited him?   For what, Paula?*" Mia asked as she closed the front door and walked back into the living room.

Mia suddenly stopped talking.   She looked at her sister and then at Jackson.

"Oh heck no, Paula! You mean to tell me, after being alone for all of these years, you decided to start dating, and this is who you chose?" Mia shouted with disgust, glaring at Jackson as if he was a piece of old chewing gum stuck on the bottom of her expensive shoe.

Jackson hung his head in shame. He wanted to cry, but he refused to give Mia the satisfaction of knowing she caused him pain.

However, he knew Mia was right.

Regardless of how hard he tried, he could not escape his past.

He was still a criminal.

As Mia continued to belittle him in front of Paula, *"The Committee"* in his head convened another emergency call meeting.

He walked away from Paula and stood in a corner of the living room.

"She has a lot of nerve talking about you, Jackson, after everything her boyfriend Daryl told you about his past. You need to shut her up right now! Go ahead! Tell her what Daryl told you!"

I can't do that, Jackson answered back to *"The Committee". I promised Daryl I would keep his confidence. I'm not throwing him under the bus just to make myself look good in front of Mia.*

The anger in Paula's voice abruptly adjourned the *"Committee"* meeting. She was furious.

"How dare you treat Jackson like this, Mia!" Paula said. *"He may not be the type of man you feel I should be dating, but he deserves better treatment from you based on the fact that he is your brother in Christ!"*

Paula was right. As a Christian, Mia owed it to Jackson to treat him with compassion, and she had done so, until about four minutes prior, when she realized he was in a relationship with her only sister.

Mia had a dilemma. She couldn't tell Paula about Jackson's criminal background, and she wasn't sure if Jackson disclosed his past to Paula and she chose to overlook it.

Mia took a deep breath to compose herself.

"Paula, I'm sorry, but I have to go. Maybe it's my overprotectiveness that's rising up; I don't know. What I do know is that I'm not feeling this relationship between you and Jackson." Mia said as she faced her younger sister.

"Paula, I love you, and I want the best for you. I want you to be happy, I really do. You worked hard to get everything you have. You went to college, earned your degree, have a wonderful career, and you own this beautiful house. You've made a life for yourself, by yourself. You deserve somebody who can bring something to the table; somebody who is going to meet you where you are," Mia said.

Paula moved away from her sister, walked over to where Jackson had been standing alone, and grabbed his hand.

"Jackson has met me where I am spiritually and emotionally. That's all that matters to me," Paula said.

"It's really nice that you feel that way, Paula, but trust me when I tell you," Mia said, glaring at Jackson one last time. *"You can do better. Much better."*

Without saying goodbye, Mia turned and walked out the front door.

The room was silent.

Neither Paula nor Jackson knew what to say or what to do.

The timer on the oven broke the silence.

Jackson turned to face Paula. *"Your sister is right, Paula. You can do better,"* he said.

"*Excuse me, Jackson. What are you saying?*" Paula asked.

"*There are some things about my past it's time you knew about,*" Jackson said.

Paula walked back into the kitchen, opened the oven door, removed a pan containing the baked potatoes, and placed it on the granite countertop. She closed the oven door and pulled the potholders from her hands.

"*Jackson, are you on Mia's caseload or something? Is that it? Is that why she was acting the way she was?*" Paula asked. "*Does she know you from her job?*"

"*No, Paula.*" Jackson answered. "*But she knew me before I came to Wayside. Look, let's fix our plates, sit down, and I'll tell you over dinner where I was when I met your sister. I knew this day was going to come. You may not want to be in a relationship with me afterward, but I pray you will at least continue to be my friend.*"

"*It's like that, Jackson?*" Paula asked.

"*Yes, Paula, it's like that, and then some,*" Jackson answered.

25

Paula eyed herself one last time in the full-length mirror before she put on her camel-colored suit jacket and walked out of her master bedroom.

It had been a week since they had spoken to each other. Paula never expected their separation to last this long.

It was worse than I thought, she said to herself as her mind traveled back to the events that had taken place at her home the previous Sunday afternoon.

Paula locked her front door and simultaneously remote-started her car.

She was at a loss for words. It was the first time in her life she and her sister had fallen out over anything. Ever since their mother passed away when they were both teenagers, nothing or no one ever came between them.

Until last Sunday afternoon, Paula did not believe anything or anyone could.

But Jackson Braynor did.

Is he worth it? Paula now asked herself.

Driving through the gates of her apartment complex, she thought about Jackson and what he had told her.

She had to admit Mia was correct: She could do better. Jackson had serious issues. Yes, he was a little *"rough around the edges";* however, he had come a long way and was working hard to change his life.

It's too late anyway; I already fell in love with him, Paula admitted to herself.

Furthermore, after listening to his life story, Paula acquired a greater appreciation for him.

Instead of Jackson's confession turning her away, it drew her closer to him.

Jackson was an overcomer; someone she was proud to know.

Mia needs to get to know him as a Christian man, not as the inmate she met at the jail. She'll change her mind, Paula thought to herself as she drove onto the church's parking lot.

Paula walked into the sanctuary and found her usual seat in Deacon Wright's Sunday School. She looked around for her sister.

Mia had not yet arrived.

About fifteen minutes after class began, Darlene Walker made her customary grand entrance. However, since their conversation in the beauty salon, Paula observed that Darlene had toned down her attire somewhat.

She was tastefully dressed in a navy blue fitted suit that was flattering but did not illicit drool from the mouths of men she encountered.

Darlene usually sat near the back, but after spotting Paula, she made her way to where she was sitting.

"Scoot over, Paula," Darlene said, smiling down at her new friend.

"Morning Darlene," Paula whispered, genuinely glad to see a friendly face. *"How have you been?"*

"Better than you, I hear," Darlene said, to Paula's surprise.

"Really? What have you heard?" Paula whispered.

"Come outside with me for a minute," Darlene said as she stood and headed toward the vestibule.

Paula rose quietly and followed Darlene. They found two overstuffed chairs in a corner facing each other hidden by large potted plants.

"Look, Paula, it's none of my business, but my brother Daryl told me what happened between you and Mia last Sunday afternoon."

"What exactly did he tell you?" Paula asked.

"He told me that Mia showed up at your apartment last week and found out that you and Jackson are seeing each other," Darlene answered with a mischievous smile.

"Girl, why didn't you tell me about Jackson last Saturday in the beauty salon when I asked you if you were seeing anybody? He's fine!" Darlene said, playfully slapping Paula's knee.

"Thanks for your endorsement, Darlene, but I'm a private person. I didn't know you well enough at the time to be telling you about my love life. Anyway, did Daryl tell you how badly Mia acted toward Jackson? She apparently

knows about Jackson's past, and is now judging him based on it," Paula said. "It's not right. Jackson is saved now."

"No, Daryl didn't mention that. He's probably afraid for the stability of his own relationship at this point," Darlene said.

"What do you mean?" Paula asked, her curiosity piqued. "I thought Daryl and Mia's relationship was strong."

Darlene suddenly looked nervous. She strained her neck a little to make sure no one was within listening distance.

She turned back and faced Paula.

"If I tell you something, you can't mention it to a soul. Not your sister or anyone," Darlene whispered.

Darlene paused again to look over the potted plants one last time for anyone within earshot.

"Something happened when we were teenagers. We never told anyone about it. I'm telling you, because you're my friend and I don't want you to let your sister make you feel guilty about your relationship with Jackson," Darlene said.

The front door to the church opened. Paula and Darlene looked through the leaves of the plants and saw Mia and Daryl enter the vestibule.

Because Paula and Darlene were secluded, Mia and Daryl could not see them huddled together in the corner. Mia and Daryl proceeded into the sanctuary.

"I really like them together," Paula said. *"I just wish she felt the same way about me and Jackson. He has issues, but he's really a good person, and he is good to me and for me."*

"Daryl is a good person, too," Darlene said. *"Mia is blessed to have him. However, everything that glitters now wasn't always gold."*

"Let me tell you what happened, Paula," Darlene said.

26

Mia and Daryl walked up the side aisle so not to disturb Deacon Wright's Sunday School class.

Upon arriving in the front of the church, Mia removed her jacket, sat on the organ bench, leaned over, and flipped the switch to turn it on.

She quickly scanned the crowd of students seated before Deacon Wright.

Surprisingly, Paula was absent.

I wonder where she is, Mia thought to herself. *She never misses Sunday School.*

At that very moment, the door to the sanctuary opened. Paula—accompanied by a smiling Jackson Braynor—strode through the door.

Mia's blood pressure immediately began to rise.

Jackson better be glad I left my gun at work, Mia said to herself, half-jokingly.

Discerning Mia's emotional struggle, Daryl walked over to her.

"Mia, you have to stop holding onto your anger and hatred. It's unhealthy and might I add, ungodly. Look at you. You're seething with anger, and look at them. They're carefree and happy. You're the only one miserable here. Let your sister and Jackson live their lives," Daryl said quietly.

"You don't understand, Daryl," Mia said through clenched teeth. *"I've been protecting her since our mother died. There are things I know that she doesn't, and I can't tell her, or you for that matter. I know what I know, and what*

I know is that she doesn't need to be with a man like Jackson. He's going to bring her down."

"How can you of all people say that, Mia? Jackson gave his life to Jesus. He's saved now. The Bible says 'If any man be in Christ, he is a new creation'. Whatever you know about him, you can't look at it anymore. You have to look at the new man," Daryl whispered.

"I don't have to do anything," Mia whispered angrily. *"That's my sister Jackson is involved with. He may have all of you fooled just because he's coming to church, but I've been working with criminals long enough to know 'game' when I see it."*

Daryl looked at Mia's face. The loathing in her eyes made him uncomfortable.

"I'm asking the Lord for forgiveness right now, Daryl, because I have to protect my sister. Trust me when I tell you, if I have my way, Jackson Braynor is not going to be around her much longer," Mia announced.

"What's that supposed to mean, Mia?" Daryl asked.

Before she could answer, Jackson walked up to Mia and extended his right hand.

"Good morning, Sister Mia. Hey Brother Daryl. Sister Mia, I know you and I had a little 'falling out' last Sunday at your sister's house, but it doesn't have anything to do with my ministry here at Wayside, does it? Jackson asked. "Can I still play the drums?"

Ignoring his hand, Mia said, "We won't be needing you today."

Confused, Jackson looked around at the unoccupied drum set.

"Who's playing today?" he asked.

"Nobody," Mia said

Daryl had enough. He turned to Jackson and told him to have a seat on the front pew.

"Mia, I need to speak with you for a moment," Daryl said as he escorted her to a small room near the band section.

"What in the world was that about?" Daryl said angrily. *"You can't treat people like that in this church. If you have issues with him or anyone, don't bring that mess in here!"*

Mia looked at Daryl. She had never seen him so heated; it was as if he took her behavior personally.

"I'm sorry. You're right, Daryl. I know better, and would act better if he was seeing anyone but my sister. I know too much about him, and I can't let it go," Mia said.

"Let me help you. God knows everything about us, but He lets it go. He looks beyond our faults every day and loves us in spite of ourselves. At least try to do the same for Jackson. He doesn't need any more people in his life reminding him of his past shortcomings, especially church folks. What he needs now is encouragement to overcome. That's what people come to church for," Daryl said.

"Daryl, I'll let him play in the band here at the church, but I'm not about to sit by and let him drag my sister down. She can do better," Mia said as she walked back into the sanctuary.

Mia found Jackson still seated on the front pew.

"Look, Jackson, I apologize for the way I acted. My negative feelings about your relationship with my sister shouldn't have followed me into church today. Both of us are here to do ministry, and that's exactly what we're going to do. You're welcome to play," Mia said.

"Thanks, Sister Mia," Jackson said. *"And for the record, I love your sister. I know you look at me a certain way because of where I was the first time we met, but I've changed. My new life is the partly the fruit of your ministry to me that evening, not only the music ministry but the things you said to me after the service. I hope one day you will see me as the person I'm becoming instead of the person I was."*

"You're asking for way too much, Jackson. Just sit down and play," Mia said.

At the end of the service—during the benediction—Paula was nervously shuffling her feet. Church was about to be over, and there was no way she was leaving without speaking to her sister.

It had been an entire week. Paula had no idea what to expect when she approached Mia after service.

Paula felt a tap on her left shoulder. She turned to find Darlene standing alongside her.

"Are you okay, Paula?" she asked.

"I need to be asking you that, Darlene." Paula responded, with concern in her voice.

"Yes, I'm okay. I'm glad to have finally shared that with someone I could trust. I've held onto it for so many years. As I've said, the only people who knew were my family

members. You're the first outsider I ever told," Darlene said.

"I'm humbled and honored that you trusted me enough to share what happened to you. You can trust me, Darlene. I will never betray your confidence, and if you ever need to talk about anything, feel free to call me. Consider me your friend, Darlene. I'll be here for you," Paula said.

"Thank you so much," Darlene said, as she reached out and embraced Paula tightly.

Oh my goodness! I picked the wrong Sunday to wear this camel-colored suit. It's going to cost a fortune to clean her makeup off of my suit jacket, Paula said to herself.

When Darlene finally released her, Paula discreetly inspected her jacket. Liquid makeup, lipstick, and eye shadow stains were present on the shoulder and lapel of her jacket.

I knew it, Paula moaned.

261

Paula walked to the front of the church, where Mia sat on the organ bench, about to turn it off.

Paula spoke as if they had been chatting all week.

"Hey Sis. See you in a few," she said casually, as she leaned in to give Mia her usual hug.

"I don't know Paula," Mia said, stuttering slightly. *"This may not be a good idea. I still need time to process all of this before the three of us get together again."*

"Oh, you don't have to worry, Mia. Jackson has to work this afternoon so it's just going to be you and me," Paula said.

"In that case, I'll see you in a few," Mia said, her mood lightening as she turned her attention back to the instruments that needed to be turned off and covered.

Paula left the church to find Jackson leaning against her car.

262

"Hello beautiful," he said.

"Hi Jackson," Paula beamed as they embraced. Now that Mia was aware of their relationship, there was no point in hiding it anymore.

"How did it go with Mia today?" Paula asked.

"A little rough at first," Jackson said, as he recalled his initial interaction with Mia.

"Daryl ended up taking her into a back room and speaking to her privately. I don't know what he said, but he got through. When she came back in the sanctuary, she had calmed down. We made it through the service without her pulling out her gun and firing off a couple of rounds in my direction, so I guess all is well," Jackson laughed.

"I'm sorry she's acting like this toward you, Jackson. Trust me, all of it isn't about you. Some of it has to do with my defiance. This is the first time I'm standing up to her and doing something contrary to her liking. She's having a serious problem handling it," Paula explained.

263

"Don't worry about me, Paula. Mia doesn't bother me at all anymore. I was worried about her getting to you. Now that you still love me with all of my issues, I don't care how Mia feels," Jackson said as he planted a kiss on Paula's cheek.

"Jackson, with what I learned today, Mia is in no position to say anything to me about you," Paula stated.

"What do you mean?" Jackson asked.

"Just trust me when I tell you. Mia needs to leave me and you alone," Paula declared.

28

Paula had enough.

She arose from her stool at the island, and took her dinner plate over to the sink to rinse it.

Her hand shook so violently, the plate slipped onto the floor and broke.

Paula finally exploded.

"Before you sit there and judge Jackson, Mia, maybe you should look at your man. Daryl isn't the angel you believe he is," Paula shouted, fed up with Mia's relentless verbal assaults on Jackson.

Mia looked up from her half-cleared dinner plate, astonished.

Apparently, Paula's *"jailbird"* boyfriend must have begun to influence her once timid sister.

Paula is out of control. I'm going to need to reel her in, Mia said to herself.

"What in the world are you talking about Paula?" Mia asked smugly.

"Oh, you don't know, do you?" Paula responded with her hands on her hips and her voice soaked in sarcasm.

Mia was furious. *How dare she talk to me in this tone?*

"Where are you going with this, Paula?" Mia demanded. *"You're the one who chose to date someone with issues, not me! So, don't even try to deflect your mess in my direction!"*

"That's where you're wrong, Mia," Paula announced, glaring at her sister.

"*Again, Paula, I don't know what you're talking about. There is no comparison between Jackson and Daryl. We fell in love with two saved but very different men,*" Mia said.

Paula walked over to the kitchen island and stood boldly before her older sister.

She looked Mia in the eye and spoke ten words that would soon topple her sister's self-righteous realm.

"*Wrong. Jackson Braynor and Daryl Walker have something in common.*"

Mia did not say another word.

She stood, walked to the front door, and left.

29

Daryl walked along the shore of the beach.

A spirit of depression was quickly engulfing him. He buried his hands deep into the pockets of his trousers. In doing so, he felt the small box that contained her engagement ring.

It was over and he knew it. Mia would never allow their relationship to continue. There was no way she would marry him now.

"Why didn't you tell me before, Daryl?" Mia shouted at him earlier, out of anger and pain. *"You allowed me to fall in love with you, knowing what you did? How could you deceive me like this?"*

Daryl could offer no excuse for withholding the information for so long from her.

Daryl walked away from the shore and rejoined Mia, who was sitting alone on the retaining wall, her bare legs dangling over the side.

Mia could barely see through the moisture that covered her eyes. She had heard countless stories during the course of her career in law enforcement, but none as personally devastating as the confession Daryl shared less than twenty minutes prior.

"I was fifteen years old when it happened," Daryl recalled. *"It was a Friday night. There was a basketball game at the high school that me and my friends wanted to go to and there was a party afterwards. So, I asked my mom if I could spend the night over my friend Kareem's house; his mom worked the night shift at the hospital so she wouldn't know what time we got in. My Mom said I could spend the night over Kareem's.*

We went to the game, and when we got to the party, even though we were too young, Kareem's older brother got us in. There was wine and beer and weed there. Kareem and I never drank or smoked before, but since it was there and we didn't want to look like punks, we started drinking and smoking, too.

All of a sudden, someone yelled, 'Five-O!' We knew what that meant. The police were coming. Everyone scattered. Me and Kareem took off running and in the mad scramble to get out of the house, we got separated. I went to his house, but he wasn't there. I sat outside for about a half hour, but he never showed up. Thinking he might have gotten arrested or something, I decided to go to my house.

Since it was about one o'clock in the morning and no one was expecting me, I didn't want to wake my mother and stepfather, so I got a crate out of the garage, stood on it, and climbed through my bedroom window. I didn't bother to turn on the light; I just took off my jacket, and threw it on the chair.

I opened my bedroom door to go to the bathroom when I heard a noise. It was coming from my sister Darlene's room. I was kinda glad to know she was still up because I wasn't ready to go to bed; I was still high. So I turned the knob, peeked in her room, and I saw him.

He was on top of her, while she struggled underneath him. His hand was covering her mouth. Her eyes were wide. Her pajama top was on, but the bottoms were on the floor by the bed.

I looked behind me and saw what I needed. It was a trophy Darlene won in a cheerleading competition. Since her school won first place, it was heavier than usual.

Darlene saw me as I approached with the trophy raised over my head. He must not have been looking in Darlene's *face, because her eyes would have told him what was coming next.*

I hit him with the trophy once. Twice. Three times. He fell over onto the floor. Darlene was splattered in blood. I must have blacked out, because as he lay on the floor, I continued to hit him.

Darlene said she was screaming, 'Stop Daryl!' She said she tried to grab my arm but I kept swinging it. My mother wasn't home; she was working a second shift that night, so Darlene ran next door, and returned with our neighbor, Mr. Willis who overpowered me and said, 'That's enough, Daryl. It's over'. He took the trophy out of my hand and called 911.

Had I just hit my stepfather three times, which stopped the sexual assault on my sister, I wouldn't have been arrested. However, since I continued after he was obviously defenseless, I was charged with manslaughter.

Yet, due to the circumstances and my age at the time, I was adjudicated a Juvenile Offender and my record was sealed. I was sent to a juvenile detention center in upstate New York until the age of eighteen. After my release, my Mom sent me and Darlene to college here in Virginia. While in college, I got saved. We decided to settle here after graduation, and I've never committed another crime."

When Daryl returned from the beach and sat down next to Mia, she was unusually quiet.   Her world was shattered. She thought she finally found a man comparable to Jayson, the closest man to perfection whom she ever met.

Daryl reached for her hand, but she pushed his away. Instead, she leapt from the retaining wall onto the sand beneath and headed toward the shore.

Her mind was scattered.

Mia was in love with Daryl Walker. He was kind, compassionate, loving, generous, and faithful.

Yes, Daryl was a Christian—a new man in Christ—but his "*old man*" took the life of another.

Mia could not believe her predicament.

She had fallen in love with a man with blood on his hands.

Can I spend the rest of my life with a man who took the life of another? Mia pondered, looking up toward heaven, praying an answer would descend instantly from the sky.

Daryl walked over to her as she silently stared out at the bay.

He knew better than to attempt to touch her. Instead, he said, "*Mia, I refuse to believe you are going to hold my past against me. I know deep down you love me, and as a Christian woman, I know you believe what the Word of God teaches about forgiveness. Furthermore, you of all people understand why I did what I did. You have a sister you would defend with your life. You have to admit that you would have reacted the same way if it had been Paula being assaulted instead of Darlene.*"

Mia remained quiet. She continued to stare at the bay.

"*Say something to me, Mia. Please tell me what you're thinking,*" Daryl begged.

"I think I want to go home," Mia said as she turned and walked away.

30

Bam, bam, bam.

He heard someone banging on his door.

Bam, bam, bam.

He picked up his phone to check the time. It was twelve-thirty-four a.m.

Who in the world is banging on my door at this hour? Jackson wondered.

Panic rose.

The police! What have I done now? Daryl mumbled to himself.

Jackson scrambled out of bed and pulled on his pants.

He ran to the door. The loud knocking continued.

Bam, bam, bam.

"Who is it?" Jackson said, trying his best not to sound terrified.

"It's Daryl."

Relieved, Jackson opened the door. Daryl burst through, his strong hands grabbing Jackson's shoulders.

"You just couldn't keep your mouth shut, could you?" Daryl yelled, his swollen eyes red with anger.

"What are you talking about, Daryl?" Jackson said as he defended himself against Daryl's surprise attack.

"I told you about my past, and apparently you told Paula. She threw it in Mia's face this evening," Daryl shouted. *"I just got finished explaining everything to Mia. She broke up with me, Jackson, and it's all your fault! I knew I shouldn't have trusted you."*

Jackson looked Daryl in the eye.

"*Bro, I didn't say a word to Paula. I swear I didn't. I promised you I would keep your confidence and I did,*" Jackson said.

"*I didn't tell anyone else,*" Daryl said angrily. "*It had to be you.*"

Daryl's accusation hurt Jackson to his core. He would never betray a confidence. Even when he was still in the streets, he was not a snitch.

Jackson was puzzled.

How in the world did Paula find out? he wondered.

In a moment of divine revelation, the answer came.

"*There's one other person,*" Jackson said. "*Your sister Darlene. She recently befriended Paula after they met at a beauty salon.* *Would she have told Paula what happened?"*

"*Oh my God!*" Daryl said as his shoulders slumped. His legs suddenly felt like rubber. Like a drunkard, he stumbled to the sofa, and buried his face in his hands.

"*Darlene never had any real female friends,*" Daryl said. "*Even when we were younger, most girls were intimidated by her beauty, believing she was 'stuck up'. It only got worse as she got older. A close friend she could confide in was the one thing Darlene always prayed for.*"

"*Apparently, she found a friend in Paula. I remember how excited she was after they chatted in the hair salon. Darlene was happy to finally have a real friend she could talk to about anything. I had no idea 'anything' would include what happened over twelve years ago,*" Daryl moaned.

Jackson stood before Daryl and said, "*I'm really sorry this happened to you, Bro. You and Mia seemed as if you had a good relationship going; I really expected to be attending a wedding eventually."*

"*So did I, Bro,*" Daryl said, as he pulled the small velvet box out of his pocket and showed Jackson the engagement ring he bought.

"*I love Mia,*" Daryl said. "*She's perfect for me. When she finally spoke to me before I dropped her at her apartment, she promised we would remain friends, but she said a relationship is out of the question. She claimed it is because of her job as a federal probation officer; however, after the way she behaved with you, I think it's much deeper than that.*"

"*Daryl, Mia seems to be self-righteous. There are a lot of people in the church like her. People who grew up living lives free of major sin. They never smoked, drank, partied, or got in trouble, so they look sideways at those of us who did. The Lord is going to have to let her fall in order to teach her about His Grace. We'll just have to pray that Mia one day learns to exhibit the agape love Paula has shown me,*" Jackson said.

That was not the response Daryl wanted to hear. All Daryl wanted was Mia's understanding and forgiveness.

When Daryl told Mia the truth about his past, he was confident she would show agape love for him.

After all, the unconditional love she had shown for Jayson, her former fiancé, was amazing. Hence, Daryl was certain it was in Mia's nature to love without limit.

However, it appeared that was not the case.

Mia's love could not reach past his faults.

Daryl apologized to Jackson for the late-night intrusion. He turned, and slowly walked out the front door to his car, which he left running in Reverend Holloway's driveway.

As Daryl sat in the driver's seat—defeated—he allowed the tears to fall from his eyes.

My beloved twin, Darlene Walker.

Your words were responsible for bringing Mia and I together, and now your words have driven us apart.

With the back of his hands, he wiped the moisture from his face.

Daryl Walker put the car in reverse, and drove off into the night.

ABOUT THE AUTHOR

Frieda Smith—a church planter—is the founder of the Rehoboth Christian Churches located in Mount Vernon, NY (Oct 2004) and Hampton, VA (Feb 2017). She serves as the pastor in the VA location.

An author, singer, musician, composer, playwright, blogger, prayer warrior, encourager, and retired probation officer, she enjoys inspiring and enriching the lives of others by any means necessary.

In September 2001 she released her debut solo recording entitled, *"Standing on the Promises of God,"* on which she sang ten of her favorite hymns.

In the Spring of 2003 she self-published her first inspirational book entitled, *"How to Successfully Break Out of Jail!"* In June of 2011, she produced and directed a gospel stage play adapted from the book.

Her second book, *"Eleven Words..."* was published by *Authorhouse* in May of 2009.

Everything Will Be All Right; An Agape Love Story—her first work of fiction—was published in March of 2015. (www.Createspace.com and www.Amazon.com).

Old Things Have Passed Away: An Agape Love Story is the second book in the series.

www.ingramcontent.com/pod-product-compliance
Lightning Source LLC
Chambersburg PA
CBHW030322200626
46816CB00006BA/1897